Praise for
MALICE IN THE HIGHLANDS

"Graham Thomas knows his Highlands, lochs, glens, and salmon fishing—and as I followed the ingenious twists and turns of his tidy plot, I felt I had been transported back to that chillingly beautiful, remote country. With its accuracy of detail, *Malice in the Highlands* is a fiercely intelligent murder mystery."

—Susan Allen Toth
Author of *England for All Seasons*

MALICE IN THE HIGHLANDS

Graham Thomas

IVY BOOKS • NEW YORK

An Ivy Book
Published by The Ballantine Publishing Group
Copyright © 1998 by Gordon Kosakoski

http://www.randomhouse.com

Library of Congress Catalog Card Number: 97-95288

ISBN 0-8041-1657-1

Manufactured in the United States of America

First Edition: March 1998

10   9   8   7   6   5   4   3   2   1

For my parents
With thanks to Kristen Busch

This day winding down now
At God speeded summer's end
In the torrent salmon sun

DYLAN THOMAS,
Author's Prologue,
Collected Poems 1934–1952

PROLOGUE

The hills loomed over the valley with the dark intensity of storm clouds. It was raining lightly and Miss Pamela Barington-Jones had to clench her teeth to keep them from chattering. The mist had thickened and drawn closer, creating a claustrophobic sense of isolation, and it occurred to her, not for the first time, that if she hadn't been so pigheaded she could have been sunning with her sister in Majorca. Suppressing a wave of self-pity, she drew herself up and straightened her shoulders. She was cold and wet and stiff from her exertions, but she was not about to throw in the sponge. After all, she reminded herself, they turn out a gritty sort of chap at the Springset School for Girls.

The rain-swollen river, stained dark with peat and lashed to a yeasty foam, looked like brown ale. She was perched on a jumble of boulders that had been placed along the riverbank to protect it from erosion. The footing was treacherous, so she took some time to position her Wellies securely before going over the sequence in her mind once again. Back, stop, pause, forward. When she was certain that she had it right, she sucked in her breath and began to flail about with her salmon rod in yet another attempt to fling her fly into the river where the salmon resided, as opposed to the bushes behind her. In a final climactic thrust, accompanied by the sort of spirited grunt usually associated with American tennis stars, she let fly. When the leaves had settled, her line looked like a cat's cradle woven amongst the brambles.

"I say," she shouted above the tumult of water. "I just can't seem to get the hang of it. Er, would you mind awfully . . . ?"

Angus MacDougall muttered darkly to himself. He was a big man and he had to stoop awkwardly in his chest-high waders to untangle the line. He had lost count of the times he had been asked to sacrifice his dignity on the altar of Miss Barington-Jones's incompetence, and it was precious little consolation to imagine, as he attempted to dislodge her fly from its thorny keep, that the large treble hook was imbedded instead in her ample haunch. He yanked on the line.

MacDougall's frustration was not due entirely to the fact that Miss Barington-Jones had no aptitude for salmon fishing; he had come to expect that. As head gillie on the Cairngorm water, perhaps the most renowned salmon fishing on the River Spey, he had witnessed an alarming decline in standards over the years. His clients nowadays were mostly yuppies and foreigners with more brass than brains. Not like the great days when the river ran silver with salmon, and a gillie and his gentleman were joined by a bond of mutual respect and a love of sport that transcended mere class distinctions.

Many of his newer clients had never even fished for

salmon before coming to Cairngorm, having been enticed by glossy magazine adverts that played up the snob appeal of a fishing holiday on a Scottish estate. It didn't usually take more than a few hours standing crotch-deep in an icy torrent, attempting to cast a three-inch fly with a double-handed rod into the teeth of a Highland gale, for the novelty to wear off. Despite these not inconsiderable handicaps, MacDougall took his responsibilities as tutor, mentor, and guardian of a venerable tradition seriously. While he couldn't guarantee a fish these days, he refused to lower his standards when it came to the practice of the art itself; he had yet to meet a guest who had not been able, either through encouragement or coercion, to master at least the rudiments of salmon-fishing technique.

That was, however, before the Coming of Barington-Jones, as MacDougall was later to think of the epochal event. As deceptively nondescript and harmless as she might appear to the world, the executive assistant (whatever that was) from Birmingham was shaping up to be his Culloden. Miss Barington-Jones, it could fairly be said, embodied ineptitude on a heroic scale. She was, in fact, completely bloody hopeless. After nearly a week she remained unable to manage a cast of more than four or five yards, which happened to be at least ten yards short of the nearest salmon. Moreover—and this in particular grated on his nerves, even more than that improbable Brum accent of hers—she seemed constantly to be staring at him with a treacly sort of smile on her face. It gave him the willies. And the fact that she was paying more than a thousand pounds a week for the privilege of fishing at Cairngorm, with absolutely nothing to show for it, offended his Scotch sensibilities. True, the river was in full spate and there was little hope of catching anything, but MacDougall was a stubborn man and refused to concede defeat.

Having recovered Miss Barington-Jones's fly, which was beginning to look the worse for the wear and tear, MacDougall approached his lady, who was waiting at the water's edge, still game if just a trifle flustered. He drew a deep breath and summoned his last reserves of equanimity. He placed his lips close to her ear so there could be no misunderstanding. "It's all a matter of timin', Miss," he said evenly. "Just remember tae pause a wee bit until the line straightens out behind you before startin' the forward stroke. Then snap the rod forward, just like I showed you, like you was hammerin' a nail at eye level wi' a double-handed hammer. And remember tae keep the line high on the backcast so you won't get hung up again."

Miss Barington-Jones stared at her gillie, wide eyed with wonder, as if he were a rare specimen of some exotic tribe. She pushed her foggy glasses back up her nose and blinked to make certain that she wasn't dreaming. Her holiday at Cairngorm was to have been the adventure of a lifetime, yet standing beside this wild Highland torrent, far removed from her familiar milieu, she felt all at sea and more than a little foolish. Miss Barington-Jones had never married and seldom had cause to regret it, but she had always been attracted to the strong, silent type, and with all this talk of rods and strokes and him standing so close now, she was finding it difficult to concentrate. She shook her head doubtfully. "I don't know. It seems so devilishly complicated."

MacDougall sighed heavily. "Just try again, Miss," he

said, prudently stepping to the side and out of the line of fire.

With a peculiar rotary motion that defied close analysis, Miss Barington-Jones began to switch her rod to and fro. Although the relationship between action and reaction was unclear, the end result of her exertions was a satisfying plop fifty feet away as her fly settled neatly into the swirling current.

MacDougall, to say the least, was astonished; Miss Barington-Jones, for her part, was ecstatic. But before either of them could utter a word, her rod bowed sharply and the reel ratchet began to screech in the characteristic manner that is music to every angler's ear. It was evident that something huge had taken hold of her fly, and Miss Barington-Jones, completely flummoxed, could do little save hold on for dear life.

"Let it run! Let it run!" MacDougall shouted, leaping instinctively into action. His mind raced at the prospect of a considerable salmon being taken at Cairngorm, with all the attendant publicity and prestige. There hadn't been many good fish in recent years because of all the netting and that damned disease he could never pronounce. From the bend in Miss Barington-Jones's rod it was obvious that she was into a good one, and he wasn't about to let her bungle it. According to tradition, a gillie was not supposed to actually play his client's fish, but he could coach, cajole, or admonish as events dictated and was expected to tail or gaff the salmon at the dénouement. MacDougall, however, had been seized by a historic sense of purpose, and even if he had to bend the rules a little, just this once, he promised himself that Miss Barington-Jones would have her salmon.

It didn't take long, running downstream with the full force of the current behind it, for the leviathan to strip the fly line from the reel. Only a few turns of white nylon backing remained on the spool, and even these were disappearing at an alarming rate. There seemed little doubt that the great beast was intent on returning nonstop to the firth.

MacDougall quickly assessed the situation. "We'll have tae run with it, Miss," he announced with grim determination, grabbing the sleeve of her Barbour and pulling her along the revetment, despite her protestations, as fast as he dared. But before they had gone more than a few yards, his boot slipped on a greasy, cantaloupe-size rock, sending him hard on his arse, and Miss Barington-Jones, an instant later, on *her* bottom.

MacDougall swore and snatched up the rod. The line had gone sickeningly slack. Hoping against hope, he scrambled to his feet, reeling frantically. To his inexpressible relief, the line tightened again, indicating that the fish was still attached, although it no longer seemed to be moving. He heaved on the rod as hard as he dared but felt only a solid, unyielding resistance. Forgetting about Miss Barington-Jones, who had begun to whimper softly, MacDougall slowly picked his way downstream amongst the rocks, keeping the line taut. He was limping slightly, conscious of his bruised buttocks, not to mention his battered pride.

Just ahead he could see a partially submerged bush where the line appeared to be snagged. Absorbed as he was in the task at hand, he did not notice that Miss Barington-Jones had rejoined the fray and was now following close behind. Upon reaching the tangle, he waded out and began to rummage about with his boot in the murky, thigh-deep water.

Suddenly, in the lee of the bush, a huge shape rolled to the surface of the river. Not quite believing his eyes, MacDougall edged closer for a better look.

It was a man, or rather a corpse, its bloated face horribly lacerated and cast a ghastly gray. The head was wrapped in a shroud of fishing line and there, securely hooked in the corner of the right eye socket, was Miss Barington-Jones's orange-and-black salmon fly.

MacDougall gaped, refusing to acknowledge that such a thing could happen at Cairngorm. Then gradually, as if awakening from a dream, he became aware that Miss Barington-Jones had begun to scream.

CHAPTER 1

Powell slowed the little roadster to a crawl and peered blearily into the gloaming. Kettle black clouds were brewing over Cromdale and the bare crests of the hills beyond the river were smeared with rain. Hardly propitious, he thought bleakly, not that he was about to complain under the circumstances. Already, the hurly-burly of London seemed light-years away. He switched on the headlamps; he knew that the turning to the Old Bridge must be nearby, but the usual landmarks seemed strangely ambiguous.

Eventually he drew up to a weathered fingerpost, its directions barely legible: OLD KINLOCHY BRIDGE, $1/2$ MILE. He swung the Triumph into a narrow lane that plunged between untidy hedgerows bordering fields of sprouting barley that, in the gloom, reminded him of an old man's unshaven stubble. Alternately braking and accelerating, he negotiated the twists and turns, wincing occasionally as the car bumped over a pothole or brushed against an overgrown branch. At the bottom of the hill he stopped, lowered his window, and leaned out. The air smelled of briar and bracken and damp earth, with a resinous hint of distant pine forests. Over the rumble of the motor came the faint sound of rushing water. He eased the car into gear, all sense of fatigue forgotten.

The grandeur of the prospect that was suddenly revealed as he rounded the final turn, although long anticipated, never failed to startle him. The strath was submerged now in bluish purple shadows, but the broad sweep of the river, seeming somehow to absorb and amplify the fading light, shone with a faintly luminous quality. Framed by steep headlands were three perfect arches of pink granite, spanning the river like the trajectory, frozen in space and time, of some leaping Brobdingnagian salmon. High on the far hillside, partially screened by a black filigree of trees, twinkled the lights of a great house. Taking it all in, Powell realized just how much he had been longing for this moment and, for the first time in a very long while, was content.

Just short of the bridge the road was blocked by a concrete barrier, in front of which was parked a rusty red Escort. Powell parked alongside and extricated himself from his car. He stretched his limbs to work out the kinks and then walked over to inspect the other car. He touched the bonnet. Cool. Not a good sign, he thought, considering the various possibilities. He zipped up his jacket against the evening chill and walked out onto the bridge.

Once the main road crossing of the River Spey near the Highland town of Kinlochy, the Old Bridge was restricted nowadays to pedestrian traffic, having been rendered redundant by a modern steel-and-concrete affair located a few miles downstream. Nevertheless, the picturesque stone bridge remained popular with tourists, nostalgia buffs, and other eccentrics who still appreciated such things.

Powell's footsteps sounded with satisfying solidity on the stonework. At the center of the bridge he stopped and leaned over the parapet. The Bridge Pool below was deserted. A short distance downstream the river turned sharply left behind an island of birch. He called out, his voice submerged in the roar of nearby rapids. He briefly considered the prospect of a stumble down the riverside path in the dark, but the siren calls of a hot bath and a whisky at the Salar Lodge had begun to beckon insistently.

Powell started back, glancing upstream as he turned. He stopped suddenly. Not more than fifty yards from the bridge, standing motionless in the streamy water, was a solitary fisherman, a ghostly figure in the gloom. Powell squinted; it was odd that he hadn't noticed him before. Presently the fisherman, who gave no sign he was aware of Powell, began to cast, awkwardly at first and then with increasing fluidity. Powell noticed that he was using a short single-handed rod, unusual on a Scottish river in the springtime. Probably a North American, he concluded, recalling vaguely that Castle Glyn had recently been taken over by a millionaire of that persuasion. Powell shivered. Must be dead keen. Suddenly there was an ominous rumble overhead and, as if on cue, the heavens opened.

As Powell dove into his car out of the rain, an old verse ran through his head:

> *Wind from the east,*
> *Fish bite least.*

Still, he thought a bit wistfully, you never know with these Highland squalls. It could blow over.

The Salar Lodge in Kinlochy was a small two-star hotel that catered largely to a sporting clientele. Built of the local stone and designed originally as a spacious private residence, it was set amidst some treed acres on the banks of the River Spey. The hotel fishing, available free of charge to guests, encompassed the stretch of river fronting the hotel and extended upstream to the Old Kinlochy Bridge and the demesne of Castle Glyn Estate, a distance of approximately two miles. The hotel water was comprised of six beats with four rods permitted on each, these being assigned by lot to guests each day. Any vacancies on the beats were offered for a daily fee to visiting anglers staying in the local area. In the autumn, shooting and stalking could be arranged.

Every spring a cosmopolitan group of anglers gathered at the Salar Lodge Hotel to fish for salmon and drink the local whisky. And while he, too, delighted in the blameless virtue of these pursuits, Detective-Chief Superintendent Erskine Powell of New Scotland Yard tended to regard such diversions as essentially means to an end. For him, the Salar Lodge represented a kind of Shangri-la, far removed from the tedium of his profession. For a fortnight each May he could forget that he was a policeman.

There is a popular misconception, derived no doubt from excessive exposure to television and the press, that police work is vividly exciting. For the modern policeman, however, the possession of Holmesian powers of deduction is a far less useful faculty than the ability to file endless reports in triplicate concerning the minutiae of bureaucratic life.

As Powell had risen through the ranks of the Criminal Investigation Department of the Metropolitan Police, he had become inexorably and inextricably mired in the administrative morass—a victim, he had finally realized when it was too late, of his own ambition. And he had long since become resigned to the fact that the job of a senior-ranking policeman had more to do with protecting the posteriors of his superiors than apprehending criminals, the latter activity apparently regarded in the rarefied echelons of the Home Office as an inconvenient, albeit necessary, evil. It was not exactly what he'd had in mind when he joined up.

There was, however, one saving grace: As a member of the Yard's Murder Squad, Powell was occasionally provided a respite from the normal routine. Traditions die hard at the Yard; still hanging in a small frame in what is quaintly, if somewhat nostalgically, referred to as the "murder room" at CID Central is a list of three senior detectives currently available on instant notice to assist provincial forces with difficult or otherwise noteworthy murder investigations. But over the years the Yard's *clients* (in the current parlance) have developed their own specialized expertise, as well as a highly developed sense of territoriality; nowadays, local chief constables are generally reluctant to call in the Yard without some ulterior, invariably political motive.

Powell had nonetheless become increasingly dependent on these fertile interludes, as he regarded them, and correspondingly resentful of the intervening droughts. The fact that he had not been called out for nearly a year had rendered the pervasive grayness of the London winter even more oppressive than usual. But eventually spring had burst forth with the eternal, if short-lived, promise of renewal, and it was with particular relish that Powell had been looking forward to his Speyside holiday. All the more so, since during the last few weeks before his departure, his wife, Marion, had not missed an opportunity to point out with relentless precision the various repairs and renovations needed around the house, not to mention the difficulty in making ends meet these days. Powell could not exactly be described as the do-it-yourself type and he was quite sensitive about his shortcomings in that area. Furthermore, he did not like to be reminded that entropy was increasing helter-skelter all around him, the existential implications of which were all too obvious.

Powell suspected that Marion, being a ruthless practitioner of domestic Thatcherism, barely tolerated his annual fishing holiday. The sole barometer by which she judged the matter was the number of salmon ultimately brought to table in relation to the capital expended to catch them—a dismal and mean equation that entirely missed the point, as far as he was concerned. And as a kind of penance for his alleged profligacy, he was expected to endure without complaint an annual family holiday at the seaside, an ordeal that he absolutely and abjectly dreaded. Lying idle on the beach at Bude while his two teenage sons, Peter and David, ardently pursued the local population of pubescent females was not exactly his idea of a jolly time.

Thus it was that as Powell pulled into the car park of the Salar Lodge Hotel, his spirits fluttered like a phoenix above the ashes of his worldly cares and responsibilities. But, as he was soon to discover, that particular species can be easily mistaken in the Highland mist for a heather-fattened grouse coasting low over a butt on the opening day of shooting season.

He was removing his bags from the boot of his car when he was hailed by a familiar voice. It was Nigel Whitely, the Salar Lodge's proprietor, hurrying over in the drizzle with an armful of logs. Well over six feet tall and thin as a stick, he resembled a graying heron. Looking a little older, Powell thought, but then aren't we all?

"It's good to see you, Nigel."

"This *is* a surprise, Mr. Powell!" Whitely exclaimed with a soft burr. "We weren't expecting you until tomorrow."

Powell smiled sheepishly. "I managed to sneak away early. I intended to call, but I'm afraid it completely slipped my mind. I hope it's not inconvenient."

Whitely grinned. "No problem at all, Mr. Powell. Your room's ready for you. I'll toss this lot on the fire and be right back to lend a hand with your kit. Bob's away for a few days so I'm more or less on my own," he added, as if by way of explanation.

Before Powell could protest, Whitely disappeared around the back of the hotel. A few moments later he returned and was relieving Powell of his fishing rod and bag. They exchanged pleasantries as Powell picked up his suitcase and followed his host into the hotel.

Powell, as always, was impressed by the care and attention to detail with which the Salar Lodge had been renovated and restored in period style by Nigel and his late wife, Margaret. Furnished with some good antiques and a modest collection of nineteenth-century Scottish oil paintings, the Salar Lodge was known as one of the finest of its kind in the Highlands. Powell was aware that the Whitelys had sunk their life savings into the project, but, in spite of a certain obvious romantic appeal, he had long suspected that the Salar Lodge was more a labor of love than a going concern. It could not have been easy for Nigel and his son, Bob, since Maggie's death, following a lingering illness, three years ago. But such was Whitely's dedication to his trade that, although Maggie was sorely missed by the hotel's regular patrons, none of the qualities of service and comfort that brought them back year after year had suffered in the least. Powell was hard pressed to think of a more fitting memorial.

After stowing his tackle in the drying room, Powell preceded Nigel into the front hall, past the main staircase on the right and the entrance to the lounge bar, through which could be seen a number of guests ensconced before the fire, enjoying a dram or two before dinner. Powell recognized a few of the regulars thus pleasantly preoccupied. At the end of the hall, situated in a small alcove beyond the dining room door on the left, and immediately to the left of the main entrance, was the front desk.

Hearing the commotion, the stout, middle-aged woman behind the counter looked up from her ledger. Her smooth face broke immediately into a smile. "Mr. Powell, it's grand to see you again! Has it really been a year?" Ruby MacGregor was the Salar Lodge's chief cook, housekeeper, mother hen, and sergeant major all rolled into one indispensable package.

"Ruby, you're a sight for sore eyes," Powell said appraisingly. "Like a rare vintage, you seem to improve with the passage of time."

"Get away with you now!" she admonished, blushing profusely.

Nigel hovered on the periphery, beaming.

Powell rummaged about in a jacket pocket. He handed her a small jar with an inscribed label affixed. "A small token of my undying devotion," he said.

She frowned as if critically considering his offering. "Well, I suppose there might be a wee treat in store for you. But only if you behave yourself, mind."

Powell winked. "Say no more, Ruby, say no more." He rubbed his hands together briskly. "Oh, by the way, Nigel," he remarked casually, "I saw Mr. Barrett's car at the Old Bridge. When did he arrive?"

"Shortly after lunch. But he wasn't here five minutes before he was out the door with his rod. You know Mr. Barrett."

All too bloody well, Powell thought with a sinking feeling. He reached for a pen and signed the guest register with a flourish. "Has he had a fish yet?" He tried to affect a suitable air of nonchalance.

"Not as far as I know," Whitely said brightly. "But then again," he added on a more sobering note, "he's not back yet."

Powell sighed and picked up his suitcase. "I'm going to get settled in. When Mr. Barrett returns, tell him I'll join him for a drink before dinner. And, Nigel—"

"Yes, Mr. Powell?"

"Wish me luck—" he smiled wanly "—I think I'm going to need it." He then turned and bounded up the stairs.

"Right." Whitely smiled, shaking his head. This obsession with fishing was quite beyond him. He failed to understand the attraction of the thing, when the same result could be obtained with a lot less bother by simply paying a visit to the fishmongers'. He supposed that one had to have a certain mental outlook to enjoy fishing, and deep down he suspected that the sport represented the fulfillment of some primal, slightly unsavory urge. Now curling, that was a different kettle of fish entirely. Still, anglers were his bread and butter, and he had to admit that he genuinely enjoyed the company of many of his regular guests, and that of Mr. Powell and Mr. Barrett in particular. Since their first meeting at the hotel several years ago, the two policemen had become fast friends and keen rivals. Their annual competition for the first, most, and biggest salmon had become something of a tradition at the Salar Lodge, with Mr. Powell being hitherto cast in the role of the underdog. But perhaps, Whitely mused, this year would be different.

When Powell came down an hour later, the first thing he noticed, resplendent on the hall table, was a salmon, not overly large but as bright as the sterling tray on which it lay and still fresh with the purplish tinge of the sea. He sighed, drew a deep breath, and, steeling himself, entered the bar expecting the worst. He was not disappointed.

At a table near the fire, a large, bearded man with a subtle peculiarity of expression that eluded exact description leapt to his feet. "A bonny fish, wouldn't you agree, Erskine?" he roared heartily.

Powell joined him and sat down, resigned now to his fate. "Hullo, Alex. I see you got lucky."

Barrett clapped Powell on the back. "Luck had nothing to do with it, man. Now if you'll just sit back and relax, I'll describe to you in precise detail how it was that I managed to capture the canny beast."

"Sniggled the poor tiddler while she was looking for her mama, I expect," Powell muttered.

"Now, Erskine, no need to get testy. If you'll just buy me a drink, I promise that tomorrow I'll show you how to catch one, too, and we needn't say another word about it."

"Great."

Powell went up to the bar. "Greetings, George. How goes the battle?"

George Stuart, former gillie at Castle Glyn, tended bar at the Salar Lodge and helped out with odd jobs. "Couldna be better, Mr. Powell." He was unable to suppress a toothless grin. "Mr. Barrett's a great one for the kiddin', wouldn't you say, sir?"

Powell smiled sourly. "I would indeed, George, but he who laughs last, eh?"

The bartender leaned closer, lowering his voice to a conspiratorial whisper. "Try a Munro Killer on a wee double. And use a floatin' line now that the water is startin' to warm up."

Powell winked. "Much appreciated, George. Now then, the same again for Mr. Barrett, the usual for me, I think, and, oh, yes, a very large one for yourself."

Stuart beamed. "My pleasure, Mr. Powell."

Powell returned with the whiskies.

"Now that we've dispensed with the usual formalities, how the hell are you, Alex?"

As they sat together in the lounge bar of the Salar Lodge, Barrett and Powell would doubtless have appeared to an observer as conspicuous opposites in temperament who seemed, nonetheless, completely at ease in each other's company. The "large Scottish gentleman"—

as he was referred to in hushed, rather reproving tones by the two sturdy ladies from Thirsk at the next table— lacked any vestige of the taciturn reserve normally attributed to his race as he held forth, gesticulating wildly to embellish some dogmatic assertion or other. His English companion, who appeared slightly older and almost excessively reserved by way of contrast, could be seen to interject only the occasional remark, the seemingly innocuous nature of which was often belied by the spirited reaction it evoked.

Later in the dining room over dessert, it occurred to Powell to mention something that had nearly slipped his mind. "I had an unexpected call last week from an old acquaintance of mine. Chap named Pinky Warburton."

"Pinky?" Barrett snorted derisively.

"A schoolboy sobriquet derived from a rather remarkable rubicundity, if you must know. His proper name is Alphonse. His mother's French."

"Oh, aye?" Barrett yawned, obviously not impressed with either the subject matter or Powell's alliterative prowess.

"His father and mine were old army chums. We used to spend a week each summer at their country place in Hampshire."

"Country place, you say? Replete with chalk-stream trout and high pheasants, no doubt. Erskine, I'm truly impressed."

Powell continued, ignoring what he had come to recognize in Barrett as a kind of reverse snobbery, "We'd managed to keep in touch over the years, but after his father died a few years ago Pinky more or less dropped out of circulation. Appearances to the contrary, it turned out that the family was actually quite hard up."

"Ah, the modern plight of the landed classes," Barrett observed pointedly.

"That's not the worst of it. After Pinky's father had somehow managed to fritter away what little remained of the family fortune, his mother ran off with a Texas millionaire. It all proved to be too much for the old boy and he eventually shot himself. Pinky took it pretty hard, as you might expect." Powell sipped his port impassively. "After death duties and the rest, he was basically left without a pot to piss in. In the end he had to sell the family holdings to settle his father's debts. Since then he's knocked about a bit, trying his hand at one thing or another, but, as I say, I hadn't heard from him for some time. Until last week."

"A tragic tale, I'll grant you, but may I inquire as to the point of it all?"

"I'm getting to that," Powell replied tersely. At times Barrett could be quite irritating. "Pinky seemed a bit down in the mouth. It wasn't anything he said, really, but I got the distinct impression that it would do him a world of good to get away for a while. To cut a long story short, I invited him up here to join us, so we'll be, ah, a threesome. I hope you don't mind, since he'll be arriving tomorrow."

"Of course not," Barrett said shortly, fixing Powell with a penetrating look. "As long as it's clearly understood that this is a fishing expedition and not some sort of soul-searching session."

Powell flushed. "Don't be ridiculous, Alex. Pinky's all right. He simply needs a brief respite from the rat race—I know I bloody well do." He yawned and consulted his watch. "Is that the time? I'd better turn in."

"At nine-thirty?" Then Barrett grinned knowingly. "The early bird catches the worm, eh?" He drained his glass. "I think I'll do the same."

"By the way, which beat did we draw?"

"Number three, which is where, as you will no doubt recall, I caught the sixteen-pounder last year."

Powell sighed and raised his glass. "Up yours, Alex."

CHAPTER 2

It rained heavily all night and when Powell came down to breakfast the next morning he encountered a general atmosphere of doom and gloom. Even Nigel seemed uncharacteristically somber. The river had risen almost two feet overnight and would probably be unfishable for at least a day, perhaps longer.

Powell located Barrett in the crowded dining room, presiding over a mountain of rashers and fried tomatoes. Amidst the clatter there was much animated discussion of weather and water conditions. Powell pulled up a chair. "It looks like I'll have bags of time to catch up on my Proust," he remarked morosely, helping himself to a cup of coffee from Barrett's carafe.

Barrett crunched noisily on a piece of toast, scattering crumbs like spindrift. "You're too easily discouraged, Erskine. I, for my part, am not about to let a little inclemency ruin my sport. As a matter of fact, in anticipation of just such a development I've brought along some fluorescent flies, which the maker assures me will positively glow in the dark. Just the thing for the prevailing murky conditions."

"You're a true fanatic, Alex. But I wish you luck."

Barrett frowned. "Luck has nothing to do with it, man—in fishing, or in any of life's more trivial endeavors for that matter."

"I'll try to remember that," Powell replied dryly, reluctantly forgoing a more satisfying rejoinder. "By the way, did you happen to notice that Nigel is looking a little down in the mouth this morning?"

"I can't imagine why. Bar profits will no doubt soar with this lot hanging about all day."

"You're also a cynic."

"Hadn't you better get on with your breakfast? Time and tide, you know."

Powell shook his head. "You carry on. I intend to stay warm and dry. Besides, I'd like to be here when Pinky arrives. He was to come up to Aviemore by train last night, so I'm expecting him before lunch."

Barrett grunted neutrally.

After breakfast Barrett, clad in oilskins, departed for his beat, leaving Powell to peruse the local newspapers. It was later that morning when Powell learned that Charles Murray, the new owner of Castle Glyn Estate, had gone missing. Ruby had appeared in an agitated state in the sitting room where Powell had secluded himself, inquiring after Chief Inspector Barrett. Her referring to Barrett thus, struck Powell as a little odd at the time.

"I've just had a call from Miss Murray at Castle Glyn," she explained breathlessly. "Her father, Mr. Murray, didna come home last night, and the poor lass is worried sick. I comforted her as best I could and promised to ask after him in the town." She hesitated and then added, almost as an afterthought, "It seemed best to inform Mr. Barrett—in case something has happened."

"Very wise, Ruby, but I'm sure there's nothing to worry about," Powell replied soothingly.

Ruby, however, did not seem reassured. It occurred to him that something was not quite right. "Did Miss Murray have some reason to think that her father was here at the hotel?" he inquired against his better judgment.

Ruby turned a telltale shade of pink and stammered, "No—I mean—well, she thought he might have stopped by last night."

"Oh, yes?"

She seemed to come to a decision. "Perhaps I shouldn't mention it, Mr. Powell, but I understand that Mr. Murray liked his whisky and, well . . ." She left the rest unsaid.

Powell sighed. It was beginning to sound all too familiar. "Ruby, would I be totally wide of the mark if I were to guess that this sort of thing has happened before?" he asked gently.

Ruby averted her eyes. "It's no' the first time, apparently."

Powell thought he detected a slight edge to her voice, and he was more than a little puzzled by her behavior, which was not in keeping with her usual equable and sensible nature. In spite of Murray's apparent penchant for drinking more than he should and spending the night where he shouldn't, perhaps, it seemed to him that she was overreacting to the situation. Maybe Murray had got himself into some sort of trouble on previous occasions. But what, he wondered, had any of it to do with Ruby?

Mentally shrugging, he said, "Well, I shouldn't be too concerned. I'm sure he'll turn up eventually. They usually do. In the meantime I'll deliver your message to Mr. Barrett. I could use the exercise."

Ruby relaxed visibly, as if a burden had been lifted. "Thank you, Mr. Powell," she said quietly.

"Don't mention it. It's the least I can do. Oh, if Mr. Warburton should arrive before I get back, look after him, would you?"

"Yes, of course, Mr. Powell."

As he left the hotel, Powell observed that it had stopped raining and a small patch of blue sky had appeared overhead. Whistling tunelessly, he set off on the half-mile walk to number three beat.

Alphonse "Pinky" Warburton arrived at the Salar Lodge with characteristic élan, skidding his rented Land Rover to an abrupt stop on the gravel sweep fronting the hotel. Short, round, and avuncular, he was turned out like a true countryman in a tweed Norfolk jacket and matching breeks, a tattersall check shirt adorned with a chartreuse tie depicting orange partridges in flight, and a commando-style sweater in which no self-respecting commando would be caught dead.

He was greeted at the front entrance by Nigel Whitely, who welcomed him to the Salar Lodge. Whitely explained that Mr. Powell had just stepped out but was expected back shortly for lunch. And would Mr. Warburton care for a complimentary aperitif while he waited?

"Sun's over the yardarm, what? Very kind of you, Whitely."

Nigel took charge of Warburton's luggage and, as they

entered the hotel, inquired if he had enjoyed a pleasant
drive from Aviemore.

"Absolutely first-rate! I departed early and proceeded
at a leisurely pace to better enjoy your magnificent Highland scenery."

"Is this your first visit to Kinlochy?"

Warburton smiled. "Not exactly. For many years my
father rented a beat on the Dee near Aboyne. As he had
business interests in Inverness at the time, we would frequently travel by way of Kinlochy and Ballater to our
fishing. I regret we never took the opportunity to stop
here, but I seem to recall that the Spey fishing was
closely preserved in those days."

Whitely nodded. "Aye, that was so until my wife and I
opened the Salar Lodge some eighteen years ago now. Of
course the Grampian Angling Association has always
permitted visitors on their water, but it tends to get a bit
crowded and, as you might expect, the fishing isn't as
good as on the private beats. Castle Glyn Estate owns the
fishing rights on our stretch of the Spey, but the former
laird—"

"*Former* laird?"

"Sadly, Sir Iain is no longer with us, but we owe to
him any small measure of success we've enjoyed. Without his assistance, none of this would have been possible.
Sir Iain believed, as we did," Whitely went on to explain,
"that Kinlochy's future was tied to tourism, so he kindly
offered to let a portion of his fishing to the hotel for the
use of our guests."

"Very decent of him, I must say. Noblesse oblige,
what? You know, Whitely, that sort of attitude is sadly

lacking nowadays, rather it's dog eat dog and every man for himself."

"I expect you're right," Nigel replied offhandedly.

"In any case," Warburton said, "you will no doubt be pleased to know that Erskine has always raved about this place. Now at long last I'm able to experience it for myself."

Nigel smiled. "Mr. Powell is perhaps too generous, but I do hope you enjoy your stay with us."

"Oh, I shall, I shall. I've absolutely no doubt about it," Warburton replied heartily.

Nigel escorted Warburton into the bar, made the appropriate introductions, and then made his way toward the kitchen with the vague intention of helping Ruby with lunch. Suddenly he stopped and frowned, realizing that he had forgotten something. He turned and retraced his steps to the front hall where he had abandoned Mr. Warburton's luggage. As he stooped to pick up the bags, the telephone jangled. It was the local police constable.

"No, I'm sorry. Mr. Barrett is not here at the moment, but I expect him back any time now. What?" He turned deathly pale. "Are you sure? Aye—aye, of course. I'll tell him."

Nigel slowly replaced the receiver, his thin face devoid of expression. At that moment Powell and Barrett came into the front hall from the drying room. At the sight of Nigel they stopped short.

"You look as if you've just seen a ghost, man!" Barrett cried. "What in heaven's name is it?"

Nigel looked up slowly. "That was Shand, the parish constable. A body has been found in the river at Cairngorm. They—they think it might be Mr. Murray."

"Murray?" Barrett glanced at Powell. "Oh, I see."

Nigel was clearly shaken by the news. He made an obvious effort to regain his composure. "I didn't really know him," he volunteered. "I mean, not very well, at any rate. But, still . . ."

Barrett took charge. "Now, there's no point in jumping to conclusions until we're in full possession of the facts. I'll have a word with Shand and get to the bottom of it. Erskine, you might as well start lunch. I shouldn't be very long."

"Oh, my goodness, I'd completely forgotten!" Nigel exclaimed, once again the solicitous host. "Mr. Warburton has arrived. He's waiting in the bar."

"Thank you, Nigel," Powell said. He turned to Barrett. "I'll leave you to it, then."

Powell and Warburton were enjoying a postprandial smoke when Barrett joined them. After the introductions Powell inquired how Barrett had got on.

"It's Murray, all right. His daughter has just made a positive ID. At approximately eleven this morning the body was fished out of the river at Cairngorm—quite literally, I might add—by a gillie named MacDougall. He'd been dead for about twelve hours, give or take."

"What's the verdict?"

Barrett shrugged. "Accidental drowning, from all appearances. It's consistent with what Ruby told you. The man probably got drunk and ended up in the river as a result of some mishap or other. Considering the height of the spate, it's a wonder he didn't finish up in the firth. Ruby was right to be concerned, as it turns out."

Powell felt the none too subtle barb. "Pinky, I do hope we're not boring you to tears," he said.

"On the contrary, I find it all quite fascinating."

Powell smiled wryly.

Warburton turned to Barrett. "I didn't realize that Kinlochy was within your precinct."

"It's not really; Grantown Subdivision covers Speyside. I work out of Divisional Headquarters in Inverness. We don't normally get involved in local matters unless we're called in. In this case the locals knew I was in the neighborhood, so I expect I was notified simply as a matter of courtesy."

"I wouldn't be too sure of that if I were you," Powell volunteered with a wicked grin. "The locals could be easily forgiven for screaming bloody blue murder for help on this one. And, as you say, you are most conveniently in the neighborhood."

Barrett glowered. "Don't be daft. I'm on holiday. And besides, the matter is strictly routine."

Powell leaned back in his chair. He was beginning to enjoy himself; it wasn't often he found himself in a position to get Barrett's goat. "Surely it hasn't escaped your attention, Alex, that there are several points in connection with this matter that are not exactly routine. First off, this was no ordinary bloke. Castle Glyn is a substantial estate, so Murray was obviously a wealthy man. He was also a foreign national—a Canadian, I believe—which lends a certain delicacy to the situation. I would humbly submit," Powell concluded, assuming the pedantic air he normally reserved for addressing cadets at the Metropolitan Police Training Centre, "that whilst a superficial examination of the circumstances might lead one to jump to certain obvious conclusions, there are numerous loose ends that remain to be tied. Altogether, I should say, a most worthy case for Chief Inspector Barrett of the Northern Constabulary."

"Bugger off."

"Right, but don't say I didn't warn you."

At that instant, the mantel clock struck one and, as if on cue, a young man entered the room. It was Bob Whitely. In his mid-twenties and tall like his father, he came over to their table, smiling engagingly. Powell introduced Warburton and after handshakes all around he invited Whitely to join them.

"Nigel tells me you've been in Aberdeen, Bob," Powell said. "Business or pleasure?"

Whitely smiled thinly. "Business, actually. I'm looking for work on the oil rigs." As if to justify himself, he continued quickly, "At my age one has to think about the future and, well, things here don't look too promising . . ." he trailed off awkwardly.

Powell was momentarily taken aback. He had always assumed that Bob would someday carry on the Whitely tradition at the Salar Lodge, but times were hard and greener pastures no doubt beckoned. He couldn't help wondering if Nigel would be able to manage on his own, should the time come. In his blandest tone he inquired about the prospects.

"Pretty grim, I'm afraid. But there may be a chance of something this summer. It apparently rather depends on the price of oil."

"Well, I wish you the best of luck, Bob."

Whitely mumbled something in reply and there was an uncomfortable silence.

No doubt thinking it advisable to change the subject,

Barrett piped in cheerily, "I expect you've heard about the drowning, Bob."

Without warning, Whitely leapt to his feet, sending his chair crashing to the floor. "Aye, and I'm sick to death of hearing about it, if you must know!" he snapped.

The clatter of utensils and murmur of voices ceased. All eyes were on Whitely.

He flushed hotly. "You must excuse me—I've work to do." Without another word he stormed out.

The sudden, inexplicable vehemence of young Whitely's outburst left the others momentarily speechless. It was Warburton who eventually broke the silence.

"I say, anyone for a spot of fishing?"

"An excellent suggestion, Pinky," Barrett replied with unconvincing heartiness. "The river is dropping more rapidly than anticipated and a fresh run of fish will no doubt have moved up with the spate."

Glancing around, Powell noticed with mild relief that the other diners were beginning to resume their normal gustatory activities.

Warburton got to his feet. "I'd better organize my tackle, then. I'll be in the drying room when you chaps are ready."

"We'll see you there shortly," Powell said.

After Warburton had departed, Powell turned to Barrett with a raised eyebrow. "As usual, I can see that tact is not one of your stronger suits."

Barrett was indignant. "How in hell was I to know he'd react like that?" Then he frowned. "Strange, though. What do you make of it?"

Powell shrugged. "I'm not sure. The lad is obviously under a considerable strain at the moment. And he's always seemed a bit moody. Still, he demonstrated a curious lack of self-control under the circumstances." Powell studied the embroidered border of the tablecloth. He wondered absently if the tiny pink roses were Maggie Whitely's handiwork. "You know, Alex," he said eventually, "I'm beginning to feel distinctly uneasy about this business."

Barrett noisily pushed his chair away from the table. "Don't borrow trouble, Erskine. Now, if I'm not mistaken, the salmon are calling."

CHAPTER 3

Ruby MacGregor hurried through the Kinlochy High Street oblivious of her surroundings. She did not see old Mrs. Grant waving to her from the doorway of the Western Isles Wool Shoppe, nor did she notice the small knot of Japanese tourists in front of Solway's House of Scones until it was too late.

The sightseers scattered like an exploding wicket as Ruby bowled through them, spilling her groceries into the road. Momentarily possessed with a sort of tunnel vision, she was preoccupied with the fate of Mr. Powell's leg of lamb as it rolled under the wheels of a passing estate car. An instant later she was apologizing profusely to her startled, but much smiling and bowing, victims. As there was no obvious damage, she hastily gathered up her packages, mumbled a final apology, and fled the scene, acutely embarrassed.

I must get a grip on myself, she thought, pausing breathlessly before entering the market square where she had parked her Mini. After paying a visit to Castle Glyn earlier, she had decided to stop in the village to do some shopping. That had been a mistake, she now realized, as she had been unable to concentrate on even the simplest tasks. Suddenly she was angry. How vexing it was that a man whom she had so despised when he was alive should continue to preoccupy her now that he was dead. She shook her head as if to distill her thoughts. Insidiously, the possible implications of recent events had begun to intrude into her consciousness, and she now experienced a growing sense of unease, like a storm brewing over a Highland loch.

When she arrived at her car she suddenly wondered if she shouldn't buy some more lamb. She didn't really feel up to it, but she *had* promised Mr. Powell. With a sigh she unlocked the passenger-side door, carefully arranged her packages on the seat, locked the door again, and then set off for the butcher shop, giving wide berth to Solway's House of Scones.

Dr. Alisdair Campbell cursed as he replaced the receiver. It was the second time this month that Morrison had canceled their weekly golf game. He wondered whom else he could call on such short notice. There was Dr. Fletcher in Aviemore, who, being retired, was usually available—he glanced at his watch—but, no, there wouldn't be enough time. He stroked his clipped mustache in a characteristic manner. He was thinking about the postmortem he had scheduled for the following morning. That Murray chap. He frowned. From all appearances it was a straightforward case. If he got started right away and there were no complications, he reckoned that he should be able to finish before seven, although he had to admit that he didn't much fancy the thought of a dissection so close to dinner. Regardless of how many one did, one never got completely used to the idea of carving an inanimate lump of meat, which had, only hours before in some cases, been a living, breathing human being with thoughts, emotions, hopes, and aspirations. The thing was, he decided pragmatically, if he got the job over with that afternoon, he might be able to squeeze in a round of golf with old Fletcher first thing in the morning. Humming to himself, he rang up the hospital to make the necessary arrangements.

Colonel John Furness, assistant chief constable of the Northern Constabulary, was fuming. It was nearly five o'clock, the time he customarily departed the office for home, and all hell was breaking loose. Only moments before he had been informed by the chief constable that a party of minor royals had departed more or less unannounced from Balmoral that afternoon—for a motor tour of Moray, for God's sake!—and that *he* would be responsible for coordinating the local security arrangements. And that wasn't the worst of it. The chief had suggested that he consult that insufferable arse from Special Branch, Smythe-Cowan or whatever in hell his name was, who'd been sent up from Glasgow to help prepare for next week's visit by the Polish Minister of Economic Development. The umbrella brigade's role in such matters, Furness had learned from hard experience, was generally along the lines of skiving, while the locals were left to do all the legwork.

He had already resigned himself to doing his bit for international relations, but this Balmoral business meant diverting even more personnel from their normal duties.

The force was hopelessly overtaxed at the moment and, in spite of the usual law-and-order rhetoric from the latest in a long line of stingy regimes, there was no relief in sight. Furness, however, remained philosophical. Governments come and go—he had seen quite a few in his time—but the civil service, thank God, abides.

To further complicate matters, earlier in the afternoon he had received an inquiry from the Secretary of State's office concerning some Canadian VIP—he riffled through his notes—a certain Charles Murray who had most inconveniently snuffed it the day before in Kinlochy. A simple case of death by misadventure, as far as he could tell, but he decided that he'd better get in touch with Chief Inspector Keith in Grantown for a full report.

He placed the call and was informed by the duty sergeant that Keith had put his back out digging his garden on the weekend and would be out of commission indefinitely. Furness then spoke to Keith's second-in-command, an Inspector Ferguson, who, he decided immediately, was a hopeless case. The man mumbled something about having received a report from the local constable in Kinlochy about Murray's death, but then had the bloody cheek to admit that he knew nothing more about it. Mounting a Herculean effort to control himself, Furness thanked him with thinly veiled sarcasm (which he suspected was wasted in any case) and rang off.

He ruminated for a moment and then began to rummage through his desk for the current duty roster. He'd be damned if he'd call HQ on this one. He ran his finger down the list. "Gordon!" he shouted, seemingly to no one in particular.

There was a scraping and scuffing in the next room

and an instant later a portly and florid sergeant materialized. Furness never ceased to be amazed by the speed at which Sergeant Gordon, in spite of his considerable bulk, could move.

"Sergeant, I see that Chief Inspectors Barrett and MacDonald are both on leave at present. Find out if either of them can be reached. It's important."

Faultlessly efficient, as always, Gordon reported in an impenetrable Glaswegian rumble, thick with glottal stops and elided labials, that Inspector MacDonald was out of the country, trekking in Bhutan, but that Chief Inspector Barrett was presently Speyside on his annual fishing holiday.

Furness remembered now. How providential. "Very good, Gordon. Get in touch with Mr. Barrett and have him call me here tonight. And, oh, yes, send out for some Chinese, would you?"

When he was alone, Furness permitted himself a fleeting smile. Barrett was not going to like this and he only wished that he could be there to see his chief inspector's reaction. In this damnable job, he thought grimly, one takes one's amusement where one can.

Powell sighed contentedly. He was a bit sore from wielding his fourteen-foot spliced-cane rod all afternoon, but that was more a result of rusty technique than anything else. By the end of the day, he had been able to Spey cast thirty or so yards of line, so he really couldn't complain. As usual, Barrett had ragged him about the old rod while showing off his own latest carbon fiber weapon. *Chacun à son goût,* Powell thought equably. He downed his whisky with a gulp.

The afternoon had not been uneventful. Although the river had not yet come into good fishing form, he'd managed to get into a salmon, but after one good run the hook had come away. As chance would have it, neither Barrett nor Warburton had touched a fish. A good omen, Powell decided, well satisfied with himself. Despite their lack of material success, they'd had a grand day on the water and, to Powell's considerable relief, Barrett and Pinky seemed to have hit it off. Salmon were showing in all the pools and if the river continued to drop and clear, conditions promised to be perfect for tomorrow.

Powell's reverie was interrupted by an increase in the intensity of Barrett's voice. The Scot was obviously warming to his subject.

"You see, Pinky, fishing differs fundamentally from both shooting and stalking, where the pheasant or stag is clearly the intended victim. In the gentle sport of angling it is the humble fisherman who is the aggrieved party." Barrett paused to light a cigarette. "Consider for a moment an unsuspecting angler, biding awhile beside a burn and innocently dangling a line to which he has attached a prized concoction of silk, fur, and feather—simply for the aesthetic pleasure that's in it, you understand. And what happens? A salmon or trout seizes the fly, with larcenous, if not murderous intent, and attempts to run off with it. Naturally, our fisherman endeavors to recover his property and if in the process he manages to capture the scaly brigand, which must then quite properly pay the ultimate price for its misdeeds, so much the better."

Warburton chuckled. "I must admit that I've never looked at it quite like that before."

"Sounds like entrapment to me," Powell observed, stifling a yawn.

Before Barrett could reply, Ruby arrived at their table laden with several steaming and fragrant dishes: a rich, red lamb *roghan josh*; a saffron-scented *pilau*; and stacks of crisp *pappadams* and fluffy *naans* accompanied by various small dishes of chutneys and pickles.

Sniffing each in turn, Powell was transported. "Absolutely brilliant, Ruby! You have surpassed yourself."

Ruby blushed, obviously well pleased. "I hope you gentlemen enjoy your dinner." It seemed that things had returned to some semblance of normality at the Salar Lodge.

After Ruby had gone, Barrett said, "Erskine, would you mind getting your snout out of the stew or whatever it is?" He shook his head sadly. "I should have known the two of you were up to something. I'd had it from a reliable source that you were seen passing Ruby a vial of some strange-looking substance the other day. I can see now that I should have put the Drug Squad on to you."

"The substance, to which you so flippantly refer, happens to be my secret *garam masala*, renowned in London curry circles and prepared especially for this occasion."

Barrett grimaced. "Quite honestly, Erskine, I don't see how you can rave about this muck."

Powell rose to the bait. "I daresay it's quite an improvement over that memorable period a few years back when Ruby was on her 'Taste of Scotland' kick. I tell you, Pinky, every meal seemed to consist entirely of sheep's entrails, assorted naughty bits, and congealed body fluids, the whole served up with lashings of stiff porridge."

"Blasphemy!" Barrett cried. "The trouble with you

English is that you lack a sense of cultural identity and consequently have never developed a truly distinctive national cuisine. With the possible exception of eggs and chips," he concluded with a triumphant smirk.

Powell hooted derisively. "Did I heard you say 'cuisine'? Pinky, you really must try the clapshot *cordon bleu* sometime. And let's not forget that traditional Scottish favorite, deep-fried Mars bar."

Warburton was laughing helplessly, tears streaming down his round, red face. "Stop, you two, please stop!" he implored.

"Now tell the truth, Pinky," Barrett said. "What's your opinion?"

Pinky dabbed at the corners of his eyes with a napkin. "I'm sorry, Alex. I must confess that I, too, am an unrepentant curry fiend. Indian army brat and whatnot. However, it does seem that, for some, curry is an acquired taste. As is haggis, I suppose," he added charitably.

"Aye, well," Barrett sighed resignedly, "in the absence of more substantial fare, I suppose I'd better tuck in so as to keep my strength up for the morrow."

Powell noted with considerable annoyance that Barrett had two huge servings of lamb and rice and had the cheek to help himself to the last *naan*, which he then used to polish his plate. After Ruby had cleared away the dishes and served coffee, they retired to the bar.

A short time after they had settled themselves in the inglenook, Bob Whitely came in and made a beeline for Barrett. He seemed more or less his old self and acted as if nothing out of the ordinary had happened that afternoon. "A Sergeant Gordon just telephoned with a message for you to call Mr. Furness. He said it was important."

Barrett frowned, avoiding Powell's eyes.

Whitely cleared his throat and continued, "I wish to apologize for my behavior at lunch. There is absolutely no excuse and, well, I hope you can see your way clear to forgive me."

"Think nothing of it, Bob," Powell said quickly. "This must be a difficult time for you."

"Aye, well, I'm sure things will work out eventually." He seemed anxious to change the subject. He turned to Barrett. "You can use the phone in the office, if you like."

"Thanks, Bob," said Barrett, springing to his feet. "This shouldn't take long," he added for Powell's benefit.

"What do you suppose that's all about?" Warburton asked.

"Oh, I expect it's nothing important," Powell replied absently. He swung his legs up onto the settle and felt for his cigarettes.

"Your friend Barrett is quite a character," Warburton ventured tentatively.

"You'll get no argument from me on that score."

Warburton leaned closer. "I say, he does get this queer look at times. It's—it's as if he's looking right through one. It's rather off-putting. Haven't you noticed?"

Powell smiled lopsidedly. "It's his left eye. Completely useless. Took a stray pellet while grouse shooting as a lad. Every once in a while he tends to go a bit cross-eyed, that's all."

Warburton seemed relieved. "That explains it. I was beginning to think it was my imagination."

"Damn useful, though," Powell mumbled.

"Beg your pardon?"

"You've heard of the 'evil eye'?"

Warburton shook his head, frowning slightly. "I'm afraid you've lost me, old boy."

Powell thought about another whisky. How many had he had? He couldn't remember. No matter. He brought his attention with some difficulty back to the subject at hand. "Look, Pinky, before I relate to you one of the most astounding feats in the annals of modern detection you must promise me that you'll not breathe a word of this to another living soul."

Warburton cocked his head warily, obviously curious, but leery of being had. "With a buildup like that I'd be a fool not to agree, wouldn't I? All right, I promise."

Powell nodded. "It happened many years ago in Edinburgh. Alex was an up-and-coming detective-sergeant at the time, and he'd been working on a case involving the theft of some paintings from the house of a certain wealthy industrialist. After a lengthy investigation he was still at loose ends, so as a last resort he assembled the suspects at the scene of the crime, hoping to bring things to a head, as it were. Dame Agatha would've been proud of him."

Powell drew on his cigarette with studied deliberation. "He'd narrowed the field down to three possibilities. There was the owner, himself, who stood to benefit from the insurance settlement. Bit of a shifty character, apparently. Then there was the wayward son, who had a penchant for gambling more than he could afford to lose. There was even a bloody butler, if you can believe it. The man had evidently developed a taste for the finer things in life, including the master's wife, who happened to be a drunk. A regular rogues' gallery, I think you'd agree."

He smiled cryptically. "To cut a long story short, the

ploy failed miserably. Alex was trying to figure out how to make a graceful exit when, as chance would have it, a gust of wind through the open window blew a speck of something into his good eye. As he was attempting to dislodge it, like this—" Powell clumsily pulled his right eyelid down to demonstrate "—he was amazed to find that for the first time since his boyhood accident he could see perfectly well with his other eye." He paused significantly for effect. "You're not going to believe this, Pinky, but Alex swears that he could see, as clearly as I can see you now, a sort of ethereal figure hovering over the assembly. And—get this—the thing was pointing an accusing finger at the son."

"Good Lord!"

"When Alex opened his good eye, the apparition vanished as suddenly as it had appeared. Always one to seize the moment, he confronted the lad, who was caught completely off guard and confessed on the spot."

Warburton was transfixed. "Absolutely incredible!"

"Wait, you haven't heard the half."

"You mean there's more?" Warburton gasped.

"The ghost or spirit or whatever in hell you'd call it— you'll never guess what, or rather who, it was."

"Don't keep me in suspense, for God's sake!"

Powell lowered his voice to a hoarse whisper. "It was the Flower of Culloden, the Bonny Prince himself."

The color had drained from Warburton's face like port from a glass, and for several seconds he seemed incapable of speaking. Eventually he managed to sputter, "You— you can't be serious!"

"If there's one thing I've learned, Pinky, it's never to underestimate the Celtic mind."

Warburton struggled to his feet. "Christ, I need another drink." The thought of Barrett communing with the Young Pretender was evidently too much for him.

He returned with the whiskies and gave Powell a resentful look. "You know I'm superstitious, you bugger."

Powell laughed. "Not to worry, Pinky, we've got only Alex's word for it."

They nursed their drinks in silence until Warburton spoke.

"Now that I have the opportunity, Erskine, I—well, I'd like to thank you for having me along. Quite honestly, I can't remember when I've enjoyed myself as much. I can see now how badly I needed to get away."

"Don't mention it, Pinky. But my motives were not entirely unselfish. It's been far too long since we've got together for a good natter."

"There's been a lot of water under the bridge, all right. But I'm pleased to see that you've enjoyed continuing success in your profession; I seem to recall that you'd just made chief inspector when we last lunched at the Savoy." He regarded Powell thoughtfully. "You know, Erskine, I've always regarded you as a kind of Prometheus in plainclothes, gallantly striving to dispel the darkness in the world—or at least your own small corner of it."

Powell smiled weakly. "I think Sisyphus is more my style." He hesitated, not quite sure how to broach a potentially delicate subject. He decided it was pointless to avoid the issue. "And you, Pinky, how have you been getting on?" It came out more awkwardly than he had hoped.

"Oh, I can't complain. You may be interested to know

that I've recently embarked on a new career as an estate agent. I've decided to specialize in sporting properties, since I've had a bit of experience in that line."

Powell searched for any sign of bitterness in Pinky's voice and was relieved to find none; if anything, there was perhaps a hint of irony. "Well, it would seem that your timing is impeccable. I understand that property sales are beginning to pick up."

Warburton smiled. "So far I've managed to keep the wolves from my door. I don't wish to seem immodest, Erskine, but I do believe that I have a certain aptitude for the profession."

Powell chuckled. "I don't doubt it for a moment, Pinky. You could charm the—"

He was interrupted by the clamorous arrival of Barrett and a uniformed police constable who appeared distinctly ill at ease. It was obvious that Barrett was not happy as he threw himself onto the settle.

"Chief Superintendent Powell and Mr. Warburton, Police Constable Shand. Sit down, Shand, and have a drink."

"Er, I'd better not, sir. Thanks all the same."

"Suit yourself. But I'll have one, if you don't mind."

"What's up?" Powell asked.

Barrett scowled. "A routine bloody accident and it seems that I'm the only one in the entire force competent to deal with it." But his expression suddenly brightened as his attention fixed on PC Shand. "I trust, however, that the good constable here will be able to do most of the legwork, leaving me ample time for more, em, rewarding pursuits."

Powell noticed that the good constable was fidgeting in his seat.

"Sir?"

"Well, Shand, what is it?" Barrett snapped.

"I thought I should tell you, sir. Dr. Campbell, the pathologist, called to advise that he's completed the postmortem. Apparently something a bit peculiar has turned up. He can make himself available at eight tomorrow morning to discuss his findings with us, if it's convenient, of course, sir. I was just about to check with Grantown when you called, but now that you're in charge, sir, I naturally assumed . . ." he trailed off lamely.

There was a deadly silence round the table. Finally, Barrett exhaled like a punctured tire. "Well, that's it then. Be here tomorrow morning at seven-thirty precisely." His manner left no doubt that PC Shand had been dismissed.

"Yes, sir." Shand jumped to his feet, mumbled a good evening, and fled the lounge bar of the Salar Lodge. He stopped at the front desk to place a call to Dr. Campbell.

Warburton took his cue and, after a decent interval, bade his companions good-night.

Powell and Barrett sat in silence for a few moments. Presently Barrett spoke. "The bet's off. After all, fair's fair."

"What?"

"You know, our fishing match. Until I get this business cleared up."

"Alex, I'm surprised at you!" Powell said, feigning dismay. "It's only sport, after all."

Barrett ignored him. "If I'm right, it shouldn't take long."

"One can only hope," Powell replied, not at all convinced.

Nigel Whitely stepped back quickly. He had been

standing behind the inglenook just outside the rear door-way to the lounge bar. He hesitated for a moment and then hurried down the corridor to a side service door. His movements were jerky, almost spastic, and his plimsolls squeaked jarringly on the lino tile.

He opened the door a few inches and listened. A damp chill seeped through the crack. He shuddered. Eventually he heard the crunch of gravel as a vehicle pulled out of the car park. He counted slowly to ten and then slipped outside, carefully shutting the door behind him.

A few moments later, a white van emerged from behind the Salar Lodge and turned into the empty street.

CHAPTER 4

Not a cloud sullied the pale blue sky as PC Shand drove Powell and Barrett into Grantown-on-Spey the next morning. As they sped through the well-kept streets, Powell was absorbed in thoughts of giant salmon swirling in sunlight-gilded pools. He imagined at that very moment that Pinky would be perfecting his casting technique under the watchful eye of Arthur Ogden, renowned authority on salmon fishing and resident angling tutor at the Salar Lodge.

Ogden had arrived late the previous evening with a group of clients for his annual spring fishing course, from which Powell himself had graduated more years ago than he cared to remember. In the conviviality of the Salar Lodge bar, Powell had offered, somewhat rashly it seemed to him now in the harsh light of morning, to accompany Barrett to see Dr. Campbell, the pathologist. It had seemed like the matey thing to do at the time, but in retrospect he had to admit that curiosity had been his true motivation. It wasn't until Barrett mentioned it that Powell had realized he would be more or less abandoning

Pinky to his own devices. Fortunately, Ogden, who had joined them for a drink, had offered to take Warburton under his wing while Barrett and Powell were otherwise engaged, thus allowing Powell's conscience to escape relatively unscathed. At breakfast that morning, Powell, feeling slightly the worse for the previous evening's festivities, had hastily explained the situation to an understanding Warburton just as PC Shand arrived to collect them.

Powell's reverie was interrupted as they drew up in front of a pleasant stone house set in a half-acre garden on a quiet street of similar houses, several of which displayed discreet signs advertising bed-and-breakfast accommodation. Barrett dispatched Shand on an errand, instructing him to return in an hour.

They were met at the door by a dour housekeeper of indeterminate age who escorted them into Dr. Campbell's study. Campbell, a dapper man with a military bearing, leapt to his feet, hand extended.

"Gentlemen, thank you for coming at this ungodly hour," he said smartly. "As I indicated to your young constable, I have a rather urgent matter to attend to later this morning and I naturally assumed that you'd wish to have my report as soon as possible."

"We do appreciate your time, Doctor," Barrett replied smoothly. "By the way, I'm Chief Inspector Barrett and this is Chief Superintendent Powell of New Scotland Yard. Mr. Powell is here to, em, study our local police methods."

Powell coughed politely.

"Splendid. Please sit down, gentlemen."

Barrett got directly to the point. "I'm given to understand that you've turned up something in the Murray postmortem. Something a bit peculiar, according to Constable Shand. We'd appreciate it if you could summarize your findings for us—in layman's terms, if at all possible." He smiled mildly.

Campbell frowned. "By all means, Chief Inspector. But first I must take issue with your constable's choice of words. 'Peculiar,' indeed!" He grimaced as if biting into something unpleasant. "In science, no finding is any more or less peculiar than any other. A fact, gentlemen, is a fact!" he declaimed climactically. He then fell silent and absently stroked his mustache.

"Quite." Barrett made a mental note to have a word with PC Shand. After a decorous interval he prompted, "You were saying, Dr. Campbell?"

Campbell, apparently mollified, cleared his throat. "In cases of this kind, one invariably approaches the problem with a working hypothesis, that is to say with some idea of the likely cause of death. Now, don't misunderstand me, gentlemen—I do not wish to imply that one prejudges the matter. I simply mean to say that one naturally looks for the obvious things first." He paused reflectively, this time to light his pipe.

Powell caught Barrett's eye.

After noisily sucking and drawing for some time, Campbell eventually seemed satisfied and resumed his lecture. "Now in this particular instance I naturally assumed that I was dealing with a man who had drowned. I was looking, therefore, for the characteristic findings that, in aggregate, are suggestive of death by drowning. These include *emphysema aquosum*, that is the hyperdistention of the pulmonary alveoli; the occurrence of a foam cap around the mouth and nostrils; the presence of water in the stomach; and, lastly, given the prevailing water temperatures, *cutis anserina,* more commonly referred to as 'gooseflesh.' I don't mind telling you, gentlemen, that I was more than a little surprised to find, with the exception of a small quantity of water in the stomach, that the usual indications of drowning were entirely absent."

Barrett was incredulous. "Are you suggesting that Murray didn't drown?"

Campbell nodded. "That is my opinion based on the information available to me."

Barrett scrutinized him intently. "Are you certain?"

"Mr. Barrett—" he sighed ponderously, affecting an air of infinite patience "—a determination of death by drowning is basically a process of elimination. The signs that I've mentioned vary considerably in their frequency of occurrence and utility; the presence or absence of any one of them cannot be considered, in and of itself, conclusive. In the end, one must rely upon the weight of the evidence."

Barrett ground his teeth. "What exactly are you saying, Dr. Campbell?"

"Simply that there are additional features in this case supporting a conclusion that the victim was already dead when his body found its way into the river."

Barrett was on the verge of asking, "Such as?" but decided on a different tack. "I understand that the victim had been rather badly knocked about," he observed casually.

"Quite so," Campbell mused. "I have some photographs here somewhere, taken *in situ*." He rummaged noisily amongst the cluttered mass of papers on his desk.

"Ah, yes, here they are, if you care to have a look at them."

He handed Barrett six color photographs depicting different aspects of a corpse, including close-ups of the head and face, lying on a cobble beach. Barrett examined them in turn and then passed them to Powell.

It was not a pretty sight. The victim's face was swollen and discolored and bore numerous yellowish abrasions. On the back of the head and neck there was an angry-looking contusion. Framed with garish incongruity in the last photograph, dangling like some bizarre punk embellishment from the corner of the corpse's right eye, was an orange-and-black salmon fly.

"Nice touch, that," Campbell remarked breezily as Powell pondered the photograph.

It struck Powell that Charles Murray must have been an imposing figure in life. Closely cropped gray hair accentuated a broad forehead and jutting jaw, and even in death his expression seemed slightly defiant. Powell returned the photographs to Barrett.

"My attention is drawn particularly to the bruise on the back of the head," Barrett said presently. "Would I be correct in assuming that it would take a blow of considerable force to effect such an injury?"

Campbell seemed mildly surprised at such a display of perceptiveness in one of his students. "Quite correct, Chief Inspector. A blunt force trauma sufficient certainly to cause concussion, but not enough to kill the victim outright. There was a small subdural hemorrhage but nothing of any significance," he added, declining to elaborate.

Barrett parried with an outflanking maneuver. "Do you

have any idea how and when these various injuries might have been inflicted?"

Check, thought Powell.

Campbell held up one of the photographs. "The numerous minor abrasions you can see on the face—here, for example—were sustained after the fact, probably as a result of the body bumping along the riverbed during the course of its downstream passage. However, the injury to the back of the head occurred prior to death, as there was ample evidence of a vital reaction."

"Are you able to fix the time of death?"

Campbell shrugged. "By the time I arrived on the scene, rigidity had set in to all the major muscle groups. That normally occurs within eight hours following death. However, the body was immersed in cold water, which retards the process. My best guess would be at least twelve hours prior to my initial examination."

"You first examined the body at approximately noon yesterday?"

Campbell nodded.

"That would put the time of death sometime before midnight on Monday?"

"Correct."

"Getting back to the cause of death, if Murray didn't drown and the head injury didn't do it, what in heaven's name *did* kill him?"

Powell smiled inwardly. Mate.

Campbell cleared his throat. "Ah, now we've come to the crux of the problem. Unfortunately, it is not possible to provide a definitive answer to your question."

Powell hastily revised his forecast to a stalemate.

"I can, however, hazard an educated guess," Campbell continued.

"Please do," Barrett said evenly.

It was obvious to Powell that Barrett was only barely able to restrain himself from pummeling the good doctor.

"Analysis of the blood indicates that the deceased was intoxicated at the time of his death. Drunk as a lord, in fact, or perhaps I should say 'laird.' Ha ha." In the conspicuous absence of any response from his audience, he continued quickly, "Let us assume that Murray had been out for a stroll along the river. It is not inconceivable, considering his state of intoxication, that he slipped and fell, striking his head on a rock. Given the combination of factors—a blow to the head that would normally be considered nonlethal, excessive alcohol consumption, and hypothermia—death could well have been the result."

"And when the river rose, the body was carried away?" Barrett ventured doubtfully.

"That would be consistent with the evidence, Chief Inspector." Campbell glanced at his watch. "I will, naturally, be submitting a full report in due course. Now, er, gentlemen, if there's nothing else . . . ?"

Barrett refused to be put off so easily. "I want to be certain that I've got this right. Are you telling me that you don't actually know the cause of death?"

Campbell clearly was beginning to get annoyed. "Let me try to put it another way, Chief Inspector. I cannot identify a single lethal event; rather I believe it was a combination of factors that ultimately led to the victim's death. If you insist on pinning me down, I would say that the most plausible hypothesis is diffuse axonal injury caused by a blow to the head, aggravated, as I've said, by alcohol and hypothermia. However, it's not something you can see under a microscope."

Barrett grunted. "Well, I suppose if that's the best you can do . . . but tell me, could the head injury have been inflicted in some other fashion, by a blunt instrument, say?"

"Anything's possible," Campbell replied shortly. He had begun to fidget.

Barrett persisted. "What about suicide?"

"By hitting himself on the back of the head? A bit difficult, I should think."

Barrett turned abruptly to Powell. "Chief Superintendent?"

Powell rather prided himself on his working knowledge of forensic pathology, and something was bothering him. "There is one thing, Dr. Campbell. I can't help wondering if there isn't a way to determine more definitively whether or not Murray was alive when he went into the river. It may prove to be an important point."

Campbell looked at Powell, as if weighing his options. "One could conduct a diatom study, I suppose," he admitted grudgingly. Anticipating the next question, he continued rapidly, as if to get the ordeal over with, "All natural bodies of water are inhabited by diatoms, a variety of microscopic algae. When water is aspirated into the lungs of a drowning person, the wee beasties are absorbed into the bloodstream and carried to various parts of the body—the long bones of the legs, for instance—wherein they are deposited. Their presence can be detected by means of a special test. Although not infallible, it is the most reliable indication of death by drowning available."

"Am I to understand, Dr. Campbell, that you failed to perform this particular test?" Barrett asked acidly, with obvious implication.

Campbell glared at him. "The test is not performed routinely, Chief Inspector, and as I was given no indication that there was anything out of the ordinary about the case, I did not consider consulting a forensic specialist."

A perfectly logical explanation, thought Powell, but Barrett had obviously struck a nerve.

"Well, then," Barrett said, "we'd better have our people in Inverness do a thorough job of it." He caught Powell's eye. "After all, we don't want to leave any loose ends dangling, do we? I'll arrange to have the body collected tomorrow."

"As you wish," Campbell said in a clipped voice. "Now, you really must excuse me, I do have another appointment."

Thus dismissed, Powell and Barrett rose to leave. "There is just one more thing," Barrett said. "Did you know Mr. Murray—on a personal basis, I mean?"

Campbell sniffed. "Never met the man. Bit of a recluse, I understand. Didn't golf. Not the sort of chap you'd expect at Castle Glyn."

"I beg your pardon?"

Campbell leapt to his feet as if a superior officer had just entered the room. "I'm sorry, gentlemen, but I really must bid you a good morning."

After they had let themselves out, Powell observed dryly, "A bit class conscious for a Scot, don't you think?"

"Pompous arse," Barrett muttered as he slammed the garden gate behind him.

PC Shand was waiting at the curb, five minutes early.

"Well, Erskine, what do you think?" Barrett asked as they approached the police car.

"I think we should repair to Solway's for a cup of tea to lubricate the little gray cells."

"Right."

As they drove off for Kinlochy, Dr. Campbell ducked out the back door with his golf bag slung over his shoulder.

"Quite honestly, Alex," Powell said, wiping a crumb from the corner of his mouth with a paper napkin, "I don't know why I'm sitting here with you, discussing a subject that does not concern me in the least. I could be fishing, you know."

"You're not serious! You're just afraid you'll miss out on something. Besides, I've known for years that you don't really come here for the fishing. That's patently obvious from your performance."

"Don't push your luck," Powell warned.

"Look at it this way, Erskine. I'm presenting you with an opportunity to fulfil your wildest fantasy: Mild-mannered English policeman holidaying in sleepy Speyside town stumbles on mysterious death of eccentric foreign millionaire—you get the idea."

"I can assure you, Alex, that my wildest fantasies do not include eccentric foreign millionaires. At least not the type you're referring to. But I must confess to being a bit puzzled about your willingness to share the glory."

Barrett sighed deeply. "Because I've reluctantly come to the conclusion that there is more to this business than meets the eye, and I feel that you could perhaps assist with some of the more, em, delicate preliminary inquiries. In an unofficial capacity, of course."

Powell shook his head in disbelief. "I think you're actually serious. Do you have any idea what would happen if your brass found out that you've asked an outsider to meddle in the case, and a Sassenach, at that? Be realistic, Alex. I have no official status here. For old times' sake I am prepared to offer an opinion if pressed, but I can't promise more than that. Besides, you seem to be forgetting that I'm on holiday."

"I'm all right, Jack, is that it? What about me? But more to the point, we have our long-term interests to consider."

Powell refused to take the bait.

"Good God! Do I need to paint a picture for you?"

"Please do."

"Considering Bob Whitely's behavior yesterday, it's likely that we'll have to make a few inquiries in that direction. But I'd prefer to, em, test the waters first, in a manner of speaking, and quite frankly, Erskine, you're in the best position to do so, having, as you say, no official ax to grind. After all, we wouldn't want to cause any needless upset, would we? I for one would like to be able to return to the Salar Lodge next year as a member in good standing. Need I say more?"

And if there are any bridges to be burned, I'll be the one left holding the match, Powell thought. He was well aware that he was being maneuvered, but he had anticipated Barrett's argument and had to admit that it had merit. Besides, he already *was* involved. From a tactical standpoint, however, he decided that it would be wise to maintain the persona of a reluctant conscript.

"Having given the matter considerable thought," he said at last, "I am prepared to assist to the limited extent that I'm able, provided it's clearly understood that there is a line over which I am not prepared to step. Agreed?"

Barrett grinned. "Agreed."

"Right. Now, then, I'd be interested to hear your thoughts on the good doctor's dissertation."

Barrett grimaced. "It's what he didn't say that's interesting." He ruminated for a moment. "The possibility that somebody could have bashed Murray on the head and left him for dead is an intriguing one, although the scenario presents certain obvious difficulties. And there is no shortage of alternate possibilities, including the one suggested by Campbell. But in the end I'm afraid it may be difficult to prove conclusively one way or the other. I think, therefore, that we shall have to look elsewhere for enlightenment."

Powell nodded. "I'm inclined to agree with you. And I think we'd better start with Charles Murray, himself. You know, it's rather odd; one gets the distinct impression that he was a disagreeable sort of character and yet, apart from the odd innuendo, we really know very little about him. I suggest we have a chat with Shand. He may be able to provide some local color." He handed the bill to Barrett and smiled. "Consultant's fee."

PC Shand paced back and forth in the Kinlochy police station, pondering his professional future. He sensed that there was more to the Murray case than met the eye. It could in fact be the opportunity he had hitherto only dreamt about, if he were given the chance. But being a realist, he had to admit that this was not very likely; important investigations were normally handled by subdivisional personnel in Grantown, and his own experience to date had consisted largely of issuing parking tickets and enforcing closing time in the local pubs. Besides, he supposed that he would be terrified of cocking it up. He'd heard through the grapevine that Chief Inspector Barrett could be an unforgiving taskmaster, and this had been amply confirmed by his own experience. Mr. Powell seemed all right, a bit posh, perhaps, but the Englishman's role in the affair was not entirely clear to him. He sat down to collect his thoughts. An instant later he leapt to his feet as Barrett and Powell strolled in, fresh from Solway's.

"At ease, Shand," Barrett said, flinging himself into the nearest chair. "Mr. Powell and I would like to pick your brain about the star of the present piece, the late Charles Murray, Esquire."

"Sir?" If PC Shand retained any lingering doubts about Powell, he wisely gave no indication.

"Just tell us as quickly and as completely as you can what you know about him."

PC Shand took a deep breath and rose to the occasion. "Well, sir," he began carefully, "Mr. Murray and his daughter moved here from Canada last summer. One day they just sort of turned up at Castle Glyn. There had been rumors that the old place had been sold to a foreigner, but I suppose most of us were expecting an oil sheik or a rock star or somebody like that. Mr. Murray seemed, well, quite ordinary, if you know what I mean. But he must have had bags of money—"

"Keep to the point, Shand," Barrett barked.

PC Shand cleared his throat nervously. "Well, as I say, sir, they hadn't been here very long. I would occasionally see Mr. Murray and Miss Murray in the High Street, shopping or what have you, but they seemed to keep to themselves mostly."

"Would you say that the Murrays were well received by the locals? I mean to say, did they more or less fit in, make friends, that sort of thing?"

"I couldn't really say, sir. Folk around here tend to be fairly hospitable, as most depend one way or another on the tourist trade. But I expect there may have been some who were not quite sure how to take them—you know, as ordinary folk or gentry. With Sir Iain Denby, the old laird, everyone knew where they stood. With the Murrays I imagine that it could have been a bit awkward at first."

Barrett grunted.

Powell leaned forward on his chair. "Tell me, Shand, did Miss Murray ever have occasion to make inquiries to the police about her father?"

Shand looked puzzled. "No, sir."

"I understand that Mr. Murray liked to take a wee drop now and then," Powell prompted.

"If he did, sir, he never got into any trouble over it." Shand suddenly looked embarrassed. "Not until now, I mean."

Powell frowned.

"Can you think of anyone who might have had something against him?" Barrett asked.

"No, sir." He thought for a moment. "Unless . . ."

"Yes?"

"Well, sir, there could be something in his past."

"I think, Shand, that any speculation along those lines is premature," Barrett said austerely. "For the time being, I'd like you to make some inquiries concerning Murray's movements on Monday. Who he was with, where he went, when he was last seen, and anything else you can think of. And, oh, yes, you'd better have another chat with that gillie at Cairngorm, just to make sure we haven't overlooked anything there." And then, as if anticipating Shand's question, he added, "I'll fix it with Grantown."

"Yes, sir!"

Powell was reminded of a hound quivering for the chase.

Barrett bounced to his feet. "I think I'd better pay a visit to Castle Glyn. You, Erskine, may have the afternoon off."

Powell caught Shand's eye and winked, much to the young constable's astonishment.

After dropping Powell and Barrett at the Salar Lodge, PC Shand set off with alacrity to begin his inquiries.

CHAPTER 5

The sun scattered light like sequins across the broad reach of river as Powell strolled along the path to his beat. He had set out from the hotel after lunch to snatch an hour or two of fishing. It was a glorious spring afternoon; green sallies of larch and feathery birches softened the stern relief of the headlands, a gentle breeze blew down the strath, and a pair of ospreys wheeled and searched overhead. Fishermen worked their beats with long rods and graceful Spey casts. Others sat on freshly painted white benches spaced at intervals along the riverbank, chatting about the prospects while waiting their turn to fish. The pervasive murmur of the river and the hum of insects created an almost overwhelming sense of tranquillity.

Powell paused to rest on a bench on a pleasant little hillock overlooking the river, settling back to observe the fisherman directly below him. Something about the man seemed familiar, but Powell, lulled by the attractiveness of his surroundings, couldn't put his finger on it. The fisherman took a step downstream after each cast and had soon worked his way down to the rapids at the lower end of the pool. Reeling in his line, he emerged from the river and then walked back along the bank until he was nearly opposite Powell again. Another man, taking his turn, stepped in at the head of the pool and began to fish.

The fisherman scrambled up the short, steep path and emerged onto the grassy verge where Powell was seated.

"Hello," he said, smiling, with a soft accent that sounded Canadian. "Do you mind?" he asked, gesturing toward the bench.

Powell smiled in return, moving his fishing bag aside. "Not at all."

"Thanks." The man propped his rod against the end of the bench and sat down.

Suddenly it occurred to Powell. It was the rod. A short, single-handed carbon fiber. He remembered the fisherman he'd seen from the Old Bridge, fishing on the estate water the evening Murray had died. His mental antennae twitched. "Any luck?" he inquired casually.

"Afraid not," the man said. "But on a glorious day like this, one doesn't really mind."

Powell nodded in assent, sizing the fellow up. Middle-aged, with a slightly tousled, boyish look and a pleasant demeanor. "How do you find the short rod?"

"I guess it comes down to what you're used to. Back home you rarely see a double-handed rod. But on a big river like the Spey I can see that the long rod would be a definite advantage. I'm John Sanders, by the way."

"Erskine Powell." They shook hands. "I saw somebody using a rod like that above the Old Bridge Monday evening," Powell said easily. "It wasn't you by any chance?"

Sanders shook his head. "That's private water, isn't it? Why do you ask?"

"No reason. It's just that it's unusual enough to see one single-handed rod on the Spey this time of year, let alone two. One gets the distinct impression that the Highlands have been invaded by North Americans."

Sanders smiled. "I don't suppose that's an oblique reference to my late compatriot, Charles Murray?"

Powell's feelers positively vibrated now. "Ah, yes, an unfortunate accident, I understand. Did you know him?"

"Are you kidding? In Canada, Charles Murray was a legend in his own time."

"What do you mean?"

"His was a classic rags-to-riches story of the type so beloved by colonials everywhere. The son of Scottish immigrants who made good and ended up laird of a Highland estate."

"He ended up dead," Powell remarked, testing the waters in his best hard-boiled manner.

"Ah, well, don't we all?"

A philosopher, no less. "Mr. Sanders . . ."

"John, please."

"Right. John. I must admit you've piqued my interest. Exactly what line of work was Murray in?"

"I suppose you could describe him as a mining magnate. He's best known for his discovery of a world-class gold deposit in northern British Columbia, which he eventually turned into Canada's richest gold mine."

"I wonder what sort of chap he was?" Powell mused offhandedly.

Sanders shrugged. "May I call you Erskine?" Powell nodded, and Sanders continued, "I knew him only by reputation, of course, but let me put it this way: Charles Murray was what is rather affectionately known in Vancouver financial circles as a 'stock promoter.' As near as I've been able to determine—and I must confess that I'm not speaking from personal experience—a stock promoter's job is to convince a lot of greedy and gullible people to buy shares in his company, with the implied but inevitably empty promise of vast riches. The particular story doesn't seem to matter, the approach is always the same. One of the most celebrated promotions in recent years—and my personal favorite, I'd have to say—involved a company that purported to manufacture an electromagnetic device for removing pubic hair. Apparently the thing produced a rather intense frisson and was quite a hit with the brokers." Sanders grinned and shook his head.

"But more often than not, it's a mining venture of some description that's being touted. It's amazing, really. A good promoter can create a sort of feeding frenzy for his stock, which of course drives up the price. At the appropriate time he sells his own shares, making a tidy profit in the process, and then moves on to some new project, rather like a honey bee flitting from one flower to the next. The promotion stops, the share price plummets when fear supersedes greed as the primary motivating factor, and the hapless investor ends up taking a bath. Generally the only thing that gets mined is the investors' pocket. It's all perfectly legal, I suppose, but whether one would describe such an individual as a pillar of the community is another matter."

"You seem to know quite a lot about it," Powell observed casually.

Sanders laughed unself-consciously. "It's part of our frontier culture."

They sat without speaking for a few moments. Then suddenly Sanders said, "This, all of this, it's so—so utterly civilized." He gestured vaguely, taking in their pastoral surroundings and the orderly progression of fishermen down the beat, managing to encompass at the same time the entire British Way of Life.

For a taste of truly refined British behavior, Powell was about to suggest an afternoon with the lads on the terraces, but why shatter the poor chap's illusions? He got to his feet. "I'd better push off. You're not staying at the Salar Lodge by any chance?"

Sanders shook his head. "I've got a bed-and-breakfast in town. I was lucky enough to get a day ticket for the hotel water."

"Well, cheers. And good luck."

"Thanks. Maybe we'll bump into each other again."

"You never know," Powell said.

As he continued along the river path, Powell reflected that his newly acquired knowledge of Murray's antecedents had considerably widened the field of possibilities. In a line of work dominated by fear and greed, as Sanders had put it, there was presumably ample scope for making enemies. Still, there was no doubt a perfectly mundane explanation for Charles Murray's death. Yet Powell could not dispel the growing feeling that there was something very peculiar about the circumstances surrounding the so-called accident. More to the point, there remained the puzzle of the fisherman he'd seen at the Old Bridge mere hours before Murray's death, the possible significance of which had, oddly enough, only just occurred to him. He supposed it might well have been Sanders, although he had no reason to doubt the man's word. For all he knew, it could have been Murray himself. In any case, it was the only real lead so far. He made a mental note to mention it to Barrett.

He arrived at his beat and put up his rod. As he switched out some line, he searched the water for the subtle surface expressions of the quieter areas behind submerged boulders, over depressions in the riverbed, and at the boundary zone between faster and slower currents where salmon prefer to lie. Employing a double-Spey cast, he placed his fly twenty yards out and slightly downstream of his position. Emptying his mind of extraneous thoughts, he felt the hidden power of the current begin to pull the line around.

When Powell got back to the Salar Lodge later that afternoon, neither Barrett nor Warburton had yet returned. He left his prize—a chunky eight-pounder—in Nigel's charge, with the assurance that it would be prominently displayed in the front hall. Then he went up to his room and rang up Marion. He reported his catch to prepare the ground, as it were, and then, inviting sympathy, explained how he had become embroiled in the Murray case. He then told her how much he missed her, followed by one or two distinctly risqué suggestions. To Powell's considerable annoyance, Marion seemed so amused by his incurable meddling, as she put it, that she completely ignored his overtures. He protested weakly that he had agreed to get involved in the case only as a favor to Alex, but she was having none of it. Eventually he gave up and, having satisfied himself that neither of his sons had done anything in his absence to disgrace the family name, rang off.

After showering, he came down and settled himself in the bar to await further developments.

He was still nursing his first pint when Barrett charged in like a wounded elephant.

"Erskine?" he roared, blinking myopically until he had become accustomed to the attenuated light. "Ah, there you are." He wore a steely smile of the type usually seen on runners-up in a beauty contest. "Nice fish," he remarked dangerously. There followed a pregnant silence.

For once, Powell thought, the tables are turned. He savored the moment before replying casually, "Very kind of you to say so, Alex. I haven't had much time to fish, but as you, yourself, are always saying, skill and experience *will* prevail."

"What were you using?" Barrett asked grudgingly.

"A Munro Killer on a wee double with a floating line. It seemed the obvious choice, considering the prevailing conditions of light and water." Strategic pause. "And how was your afternoon?"

Barrett eyed Powell's beer. "That looks good," he said.

Powell sighed. He should have known that it wouldn't last. There was no one in attendance at the bar so he drew two pints and chalked them up.

Barrett took a lengthy sip and smacked his lips appreciatively. He took another drink and seemed about to repeat the process, but Powell could stand it no longer.

"Well?"

"Well, what?" Barrett inquired innocently. Silence. "Oh, I see! I didn't think you'd wish to be bothered with the mundane details of a working man's day. You are, after all, on holiday."

"Cut the crap, Alex."

"Okay, okay." He took one more quaff for good measure. "I've just had a most informative chat with Heather Murray. She's quite a lass, that one," he added without elaborating. "I explained to her that we were treating her father's death as an accident, but as a matter of routine procedure we had to eliminate any other possibilities. I must say that she was very forthright. It seems that over the years her father had been engaged in a number of penny share schemes involving Canadian gold mining companies. Reading between the lines, I can only assume that some of these, em, enterprises were a bit dubious."

"So I understand." Powell related the details of his conversation with John Sanders.

"That is certainly consistent with Miss Murray's statement, although, not surprisingly, she didn't put it quite so bluntly. In any case, it seems that Charles Murray's enemies were legion. According to Miss Murray, he used to receive threatening telephone calls and letters on a fairly regular basis back in Canada from dissatisfied shareholders and the like. Mostly anonymous, of course."

"Not very helpful, then."

"Still, it's worth following up." Barrett paused once again to wet his whistle. "And it just so happens," he continued eventually, looking like the cat that just devoured the canary, "Murray had a visitor this past weekend."

"Who?"

"A certain Oliver Pickens. He and Murray were old mates. In fact, Pickens used to work for Murray. Miss Murray was away for the weekend—in Pitlochry with a friend—but, according to the butler, Pickens arrived at Castle Glyn on Friday afternoon shortly after Miss Murray had departed. Furthermore, Miss Murray maintains that neither Pickens nor her father were at Castle Glyn when she returned late Monday. She—"

"Er, I neglected to mention it earlier," Powell interjected, "but I saw somebody fishing on the estate water, just above the Old Bridge, Monday evening around six o'clock. You didn't happen to see anybody when you were down there, did you?"

"Bloody hell!" Barrett exploded. "Why didn't you tell me this before?"

"Actually, its possible significance only just occurred to me this afternoon. I suppose I've had my mind on other things." He added a trifle defensively, "Like enjoying my holiday."

Barrett glowered. "I feel like a damned fool. I could have asked Ross about it." He drained his glass with a prodigious gulp.

"Ross?"

"Murray's butler, Donald Ross." He glared at Powell. "But first another drink—a real one this time."

Powell went up to the bar and returned with two whiskies. Barrett nosed the glass and after his first lingering sip mellowed perceptibly. "Oh, aye, a hint of smoke with just the slightest undertone of melon. An excellent choice, Erskine." He placed his glass on the table and leaned forward. "According to Ross, Pickens and Murray left Castle Glyn together shortly after one o'clock on Monday afternoon. Ross was given to understand that Murray was driving Pickens to Aviemore to put him on a train. He claims that he was given the evening off and never saw his master again. He says that he spent the night in Kinlochy with his mother, who must be an ancient bird indeed, since Ross, himself, is no spring chicken." He picked up his glass. "The curious thing is, when Ross returned to Castle Glyn the next morning, Murray's car was in its usual place in the garage. Unfortunately, the gardener-cum-handyman, one Jimmy Sinclair, is apparently a member of that dying breed, an employee with initiative. The first thing he did Tuesday morning when he reported to work was to wash and polish his employer's Mercedes. Force of habit, he told me. In any case the damn thing's as clean as a whistle inside and out, not a dab anywhere."

"Interesting. What about the other domestics?"

"The housemaid, a Miss Morrow, confirms Ross's statement. She lives out in Dulnay Bridge. She says she left Castle Glyn at four o'clock on Monday afternoon, her usual time, and it was Sinclair's regular day off."

"So it seems there was nobody around at the critical time. Coincidence?"

Barrett shrugged. "I get the impression that Murray ran a rather informal household. Did all the cooking himself and, according to Miss Murray, would often dismiss the staff on a whim. Apparently he didn't feel comfortable with domestics around the place and preferred to rattle around on his own."

"Besides Pickens, have there been any other visitors to Castle Glyn recently?"

"Some reporter was caught snooping around last week, trying to get an interview with Murray."

"What about yesterday?"

"Funny you should ask. According to Ross, Ruby paid a visit early yesterday afternoon and then Nigel turned up rather late in the evening. To offer their condolences, presumably. Though I wonder," he mused, "why they didn't call together."

Powell leaned back in his chair and closed his eyes. He felt a pleasant sense of warmth radiating from the center of his being to his farthest extremities. Rather like some sort of transcendental experience, he imagined, or, more likely, it was the malt beginning to do its benign work. Eventually he spoke, "I assume that you've put the word out on Pickens?"

Barrett nodded. "It shouldn't take too long to find him." He cleared his throat self-consciously. "I've, em, been thinking, Erskine, there's really not much more I can do here at present. I think it might be best if I were to return to Inverness for a few days to do a bit of checking into Murray's background. You could carry on here until I get back," he added with studied nonchalance.

Powell was wary. "Do as you like. I suppose you feel lost without that damned computer of yours."

Barrett smiled broadly. "One of these days, Erskine, you'll realize that the information highway is the way of the future for the modern policeman."

Powell sighed. "God help us, then." He had a sneaking hunch that Charles Murray wasn't the only subject that Barrett planned to delve into while away in the big city; he had managed to glean from his sources that the Scot had a keen appetite for the lassies.

"Seriously, Erskine, I do appreciate your help and if there's anything I can do, anything at all . . ."

Powell brightened, then drained his glass with a flourish. "Very kind of you to offer, Alex. I think a wee splash of the Cragganmore would do nicely. For starters."

Under the circumstances, Barrett was more than happy to oblige.

CHAPTER 6

Powell took advantage of the hiatus afforded by Barrett's departure and spent the next day fishing with Pinky. He suspected that it might be the last chance he would get for a while. And besides, a salmon or two in Barrett's absence would serve him right; more important, it would set the right psychological tone for the eventual resumption of their fishing match. They flogged the water hard all day and, although conditions seemed near perfect, neither man touched a fish. Not a good omen, Powell concluded uneasily, always one to read the entrails of everyday events.

The following morning the report from the forensic pathologist in Inverness was delivered by PC Shand. Powell leafed through the slim typewritten document until he found what he was looking for. The results of the diatom test were positive, indicating that Charles Murray had died by drowning. "So it is murder after all," he said, feeling curiously energized.

"Well, sir, it seems a reasonable enough conclusion," PC Shand agreed tentatively. "But isn't there a more

straightforward explanation?" Mr. Powell wasn't offi-
cially assigned the case, Shand thought by way of ratio-
nalization, so it wasn't as if he were questioning a
superior's judgment; it was more like a friendly chat between colleagues, a prospect he found exhilarating.

"Go on," said Powell, rather enjoying himself as well.

"Well, sir, we know that Murray had been drinking on
the night in question. Perhaps he had an accident, or
maybe he decided to end it all and jump off a bridge."

Powell leaned back in his chair. "Taking the possibility of an accident first," he began comfortably, "let us
assume for the sake of argument that Charles Murray had
some reason to be out walking alone by the river in the
rain that night. How might he have come to grief? Perhaps he simply fell and struck his head, an unfortunate
mishap as you suggest. The forensic evidence does indicate that he received a blow to the back of the head sufficient to render him unconscious. So far so good. But one
would normally expect a person falling backward as a result of his feet slipping out from under him to land hard
on his arse or back. And one wouldn't be at all surprised
if he were to injure an elbow or a wrist while attempting
to break the fall. It is in fact difficult to conceive how he
could strike his head by falling, as hard as Murray was
struck, without sustaining other minor scrapes and
bruises in the process. Yet, according to Dr. Campbell,
the contusion on the back of the head was the only visible
injury occurring prior to death."

PC Shand listened with rapt attention.

"The same difficulty arises when one considers the
possibility of suicide. Jumping off a bridge, for instance.

But if one accepts the possibility that Murray was murdered, it all begins to make sense."

Shand coughed politely as if he were about to say something, but he apparently thought better of it.

"Suppose Murray accompanied someone down to the river on some pretext or other," Powell continued. "When the opportunity arose, his assailant bashed him on the head and then chucked him into the drink, hoping that when the body eventually turned up it would look like an accident. Thus the significance of the diatom test."

PC Shand wore a puzzled expression.

Powell explained patiently, "Look, if the test had been negative, suggesting that Murray had died before going into the river, we would have been left to account for some rather improbable behavior on the part of our hypothetical assailant."

"I'm still not sure I follow you, sir."

Powell sighed. "Why would anybody leave their victim lying unconscious on the riverbank to be discovered by the next passerby? The killer could not have been certain that the river would subsequently flood to conceal his crime. No, I'm afraid that we'd have been left with the unavoidable, however unsatisfying, conclusion of accidental death. So it is fortuitous, if I may put it that way, that Murray was still alive when he was pushed or dragged into the water."

PC Shand nodded his head doubtfully. "Yes, I think I understand now, sir." Actually, it seemed to him that Powell's reasoning was somewhat elliptical, but he wisely chose not to pursue the point. "Maybe the act was committed in the heat of the moment, a crime of passion, like."

The constable's boyish enthusiasm was beginning to wear a bit thin. "That's possible, of course," Powell said crisply. "Now, then, how are you getting on with your own inquiries?"

PC Shand drew himself up and cleared his throat. "Well, sir, I've had a wee chat with MacDougall, the gillie at Cairngorm who found the body. Nothing new there, I'm afraid. The man seemed more concerned with avoiding further publicity than answering my questions."

Powell could well imagine. "Any news of the elusive Oliver Pickens?"

"Not yet, sir. We've checked with British Rail at Aviemore. None of the staff on duty Monday afternoon have any recollection of anyone matching either Murray's or Pickens's description. It seems fairly certain that Pickens did not buy a ticket at Aviemore. He may have had a return ticket, or possibly a BritRail pass. In either case, he could have boarded a train without direct contact with station personnel. We're presently checking all departures from Aviemore on Monday and interviewing all employees who might have come in contact with him along the line. We're also making inquiries at the local taxi stands, coach lines, car rental agencies—you know, the usual routine, sir."

Powell suppressed a smile. The young constable had taken to his task like a salmon to a burn. "I don't doubt something will turn up eventually."

"I hope so, sir. I've still not been able to come up with anyone who saw either of them after they left Castle Glyn."

"Well, carry on. It's early innings yet."

"Very good, sir. I'd best be off then." Shand paused a little awkwardly. "Will there be anything else, Mr. Powell?"

Powell smiled. "I expect you're wondering what any of this has to do with me?"

"I haven't given it much thought, sir. I suppose I've just assumed that Mr. Barrett is consulting you on the case."

This lad will go far, Powell thought. He then explained how he saw his role, mainly to put the young constable at ease so he wouldn't feel he was being pulled in two directions at once. Powell was left with the distinct impression, however, that the young constable was quite happy with the present arrangement. Recalling the early days of his own career, Powell supposed, somewhat immodestly, that Shand was more or less enamored with the prospect of associating with the Yard, however tangentially.

When he was alone, Powell considered his next move. It seemed almost certain now that Charles Murray had been murdered, although admittedly, the evidence remained largely circumstantial. He was scheduled to return to London the following Saturday, which gave him a week at the outside and lent an urgency to the proceedings. For a variety of reasons, not the least of which was his sense of protocol, he decided with little enthusiasm that he had better begin with Nigel.

It was a cool morning with a pale sun in a watery sky. The distant outline of the hills was softly indistinct in the mist, lending a Turneresque quality to the landscape.

There was a heavy dew, and it didn't take long for Powell's brogues to become soaked as he walked across the broad sweep of lawn that separated the Salar Lodge from the river. He steered a course toward an island of shrubs, amongst which a tall, stooped figure could be seen digging energetically.

"Good morning, Nigel."

"Oh, hello, Mr. Powell." Whitely paused, mopping his brow with his sleeve. He was bent over his spade like a mantis clutching some hapless stick insect. "Out for a morning stroll, are we?"

"Actually, Nigel, I'd like to have a word with you, if it's convenient."

"Of course." Nigel straightened, wincing noticeably. "Getting old," he muttered to no one in particular. "Now, what can I do for you, Mr. Powell?"

"It's about Charles Murray."

There was a barely perceptible hesitation. "Oh, aye?"

"You know that Mr. Barrett has had to return to Inverness for a few days to further investigate this business." Powell smiled ruefully. "Mr. Barrett has most ungraciously refused to acknowledge any fish I may be fortunate enough to catch while he's away, so I've decided to poke around a bit on my own to see if I can come up with anything that might help things along. The sooner this thing is cleared up, you see, the sooner we can both get back to our fishing."

"I take it that Mr. Murray's death is being treated as something more than an accident," Nigel said slowly, without any particular inflection.

Powell chose his words carefully. "The police have to take all possibilities into account, Nigel."

Whitely remained impassive. "Forgive me, Mr. Powell, but I don't see what any of this has to do with me."

"As a starting point, I'm trying to put together a mental picture of Charles Murray, and I was hoping you'd be able to help."

Nigel shrugged. "I'm afraid I didn't know him very well. They—he and his daughter, I mean—hadn't been here very long."

"I understand that Mr. Murray would occasionally stop by the hotel."

"Not often."

"Do you recall the last time he was here?"

Whitely frowned as if searching his memory. "Why do you ask—is it important?"

"I'm just trying to learn something of his habits," Powell said easily. "Where he went, what he did, whom he associated with, that sort of thing."

"Like I told you, Mr. Powell, I didn't know him very well."

That seemed definite enough. "Can you tell me anything about his daughter, then—Heather, isn't it?"

Whitely's features softened for an instant. "She—" He stopped short.

"Yes?"

"She used to come by now and then to visit Ruby."

"Used to?"

"I mean, before the, ah, accident."

"Have you seen Miss Murray recently?"

"I went to see her on Tuesday evening. To pay my respects."

"Oh, yes?"

"She is a neighbor and I felt it was the least I could do."

"Yes, of course." Powell had the rather disquieting impression that Nigel was not being altogether forthright. He decided to take a more direct line. "Nigel, I understand that you and Murray had a business relationship of sorts."

Whitely stiffened. "What do you mean?"

"Don't you lease the fishing rights for the hotel from Castle Glyn?"

Whitely seemed to relax slightly. "Yes, that's so. But it's a long-standing agreement that predates Mr. Murray's tenure."

"I see." Powell quickly considered the situation and came to a decision. "Thank you, Nigel. I won't keep you from your gardening any longer. You've been most helpful. If you happen to think of anything else . . ."

Whitely refused to meet his eye. "Yes, of course, Mr. Powell," he murmured.

As Powell walked along the river path it was clear to him that his attempt at a casual chat with Nigel had been an unmitigated disaster. Nigel's manner had been stiff and defensive, if not actually evasive. It was possible, of course, that he simply felt uncomfortable, as most people do, being questioned by a policeman, unofficially or otherwise. Powell could not deny that he had slipped more or less unconsciously into the role of interrogator, and a singularly inept one at that. He found himself in an extremely awkward position: Nigel was his host and, in a very real sense, a friend, but he was finding it impossible to suppress his professional curiosity, not to mention a rather vivid imagination. He suddenly recalled the stinging accuracy of Marion's assertion that he was an incorrigible busybody. He swore aloud. That settled it; he was going fishing and to hell with Barrett.

Unfortunately, as is often the case when one is feeling hard done by, things went from bad to worse for Powell that day. He fished without success all morning, he was late returning to the hotel for lunch and had to settle for a sandwich, and later in the day, while attempting a prodigious cast to cover a distant fish, the top section of his beloved cane rod snapped off. He had a spare top back at the hotel, but he knew that the day was soon coming when he would have to retire his old friend and resort to one of the new, mass-produced, space-age articles—all efficiency and no soul. He returned to the hotel in a foul mood.

En route to the bar, he was intercepted by Ruby with a message from Barrett, asking him to call immediately, which, as it happened, suited his purposes admirably. He'd bloody well get it over with. He went up to his room and placed the call. But before he could take the offensive, Barrett had launched a preemptive strike.

"We've had a veritable spate of inquiries from the Scottish Office about the Murray case. The Canadian ambassador has been raising a carfluffle. He's even had the bloody cheek to question our progress to date, and I don't need to tell you who's been taking the brunt of it. The fiscal has reviewed the matter and has instructed us to step up the investigation."

Powell, who had never really bothered to delve into the arcane peculiarities of Scottish law, knew that the procurator fiscal was something like a cross between an English coroner and public prosecutor.

"And I've had a word with the brass," Barrett continued. "Owing to the possible, em, diplomatic ramifications, we've put in a formal request to the Yard for assistance. Naturally your name came up—since you happen to be in the neighborhood, so to speak—and, well, the chief jumped at the suggestion. We've put a word in with the Home Office and it's all fixed."

Powell could not believe his ears. For several seconds he was at a loss for words. He finally exploded, "How dare you involve me like this? You're not only presumptuous, you're bloody impertinent!" But even as he uttered the words he felt faintly ridiculous. After all, he hadn't exactly been dragged into the thing kicking and screaming.

There was dead silence on the other end of the line. Eventually, Barrett said neutrally, "Not having a great day, I take it."

Deflated, Powell described his interview with Nigel.

"See here, Erskine, I understand completely," Barrett said soothingly. "Just between you and me, I've been feeling a wee bit guilty about the difficult position I've put you in. So I thought to myself, 'Why not make it official?' "

Why not, indeed? It occurred to Powell that a rather more likely explanation for this latest ploy was to get the politicos off the local backs and onto his own. He had to smile in spite of himself. However else they might be described, fishing holidays with Barrett were never dull.

CHAPTER 7

The call came at eight o'clock the next morning from Sir Henry Merriman, assistant commissioner of the Metropolitan Police. Sir Henry was not exactly an endearing character, having risen to his present lofty status by virtue of a singular talent, it was widely held amongst his subordinates, for arse licking. Sir Henry proceeded to inform Powell that his leave was forthwith canceled and, at the specific instruction of the Home Secretary, he was to assist the Scottish authorities with their inquiry into the death of Charles Murray. His tone, however, left little doubt that he considered Powell unworthy of such distinction.

Powell was to liaise directly with the local investigating officer-in-charge, while keeping Sir Henry fully briefed. Powell's role in the matter was to be purely advisory, of course, and discretion was the order of the day. We don't want to ruffle any sporrans, do we? Ha ha. And, oh, yes, the Home Secretary had taken a personal interest in the case and was looking forward to a speedy resolution. In other words, Powell thought grimly as he disconnected, my balls are on the block. He was beginning to wonder what he had got himself into.

For the time being, he and Barrett had agreed to operate more or less independently, employing evening telephone sessions to compare notes. Barrett was still awaiting word from the Canadian authorities on Charles Murray, and the search for Oliver Pickens, who had apparently vanished into thin air, had been stepped up. For his part, Powell could now begin in earnest to investigate the circumstances surrounding Murray's death. Barrett had readily agreed to Powell's suggestion that PC Shand be assigned to the case on a full-time basis. Although inexperienced, the lad seemed both keen and capable, and he was, to some extent, a known quantity; Powell didn't need any surprises in that line.

After breakfast, Powell set out to locate Ruby. It was high time, he decided, they had a heart-to-heart. He eventually located her folding sheets in the laundry room. She started with a tiny squeak when he spoke her name.

"Ruby, what's wrong?"

She quickly wiped her cheek, looking annoyed with herself. "Oh, I'm fine. Just having a wee bubble, that's all."

"I wanted to have a word with you, but perhaps some other time . . ."

She shook her head. "Really, Mr. Powell, I'm all right. It's just that, well, it's all been rather upsetting."

He nodded, regarding her with fond concern. Although he had no evidence to suggest otherwise, he had often wondered if Ruby's relationship with Nigel was simply that of employee and employer. In any case, he had no doubt that since Maggie Whitely's death, Ruby had been the mortar that held things together at the Salar Lodge.

"Ruby, I should tell you that I've been ordered by my superiors to assist Mr. Barrett with the investigation of Mr. Murray's death."

If he had expected some sort of reaction, he would have been disappointed. In fact, Ruby seemed incapable of any reaction at all. Her expression was devoid of emotion, bereft of hope.

"I see," she said eventually in a barely audible voice.

Powell measured his words carefully. "This isn't easy for me, Ruby. I hardly need to tell you that I consider you a dear friend and the last thing I want to do is upset you, but as a policeman I have to ask certain questions." He paused to let the import of his words sink in before continuing. "On Tuesday morning you told me that Miss Murray called the hotel asking after her father. I must admit that it struck me as a bit odd at the time. Why would she call here, and not the police, if she were concerned about his welfare?"

"I really couldna say, Mr. Powell," Ruby replied, a little too quickly, Powell thought.

Obviously distraught, she began wringing her hands.

"Might it have had something to do with his drinking?"

"Sir?" She seemed puzzled.

"Correct me if I'm wrong, Ruby, but I got the distinct impression from you that Mr. Murray was not averse to a wee drop now and then."

As if to busy her hands, she returned to her folding.

"Ruby, it's important."

"I—I canna remember exactly what I said now."

Powell surmised that she probably felt uncomfortable

telling tales out of school. "We know from the post-mortem that Mr. Murray had been drinking on the night in question. I'm simply trying to trace the sequence of events, that's all."

"Oh, I see."

Changing the subject, he said gently, "Have you spoken to Miss Murray recently?"

"I went to see her—on Tuesday, I think it was—to see if she needed anything."

"Did you go alone?"

"Aye."

He thought he detected something in her voice. "What about Nigel and Bob? I thought perhaps you might have called on Miss Murray together?"

She stammered, "Oh! It—it would have been too much, wouldn't it? I mean, so many visitors all at once, after such a shock."

She had obviously been caught off guard by this suggestion, but Powell gave no sign he had noticed.

"Yes, I suppose you're right. Getting back to Mr. Murray, do you recall the last time he stopped by the hotel?"

She appeared to give the matter considerable thought.

"Miss Murray apparently thought he might have been here Monday evening," he prompted.

"I really couldna say, Mr. Powell. Monday night is my Women's Rural Institute meeting. I didna get back 'til after eleven."

"I see." He drew a shallow breath. "Ruby, is there anything you can tell me, anything at all that might help me get to the bottom of this business?"

She looked at him imploringly, as if seeking forbearance, before replying ambiguously, "I canna see how I can help."

It was obvious to Powell that the point of diminishing returns was rapidly approaching and he needed time to think. He patted her arm and smiled warmly, but to no effect.

Preoccupied, he made his way to the front hall. Almost certainly Ruby, like Nigel, knew more than she was letting on. But why would either of them wish to conceal anything? Since the murder, it had struck him that there was a fragile pretense of normality surrounding the daily activities at the Salar Lodge, but there was something else lurking not far beneath the surface.

He felt like a rock climber groping for an unseen handhold.

Nigel was in attendance at the front desk. He looked up from his paperwork. "Good morning, Mr. Powell," he said cheerily. If he was harboring any resentment from the day before, he gave no indication.

"Hello, Nigel. How's fishing?"

"Getting better every day. There were three fish taken yesterday and two have been brought in already this morning. You really should try to get out, Mr. Powell."

"Not possible, I'm afraid. It's now official," he added blandly. "I've been ordered by my superiors to assist Mr. Barrett with the Murray investigation."

There was no reaction.

"Which creates a bit of a problem . . ."

Silence.

"For Mr. Warburton."

"Oh, I see what you mean."

"But I think I have a possible solution. The other day I bumped into a chap on number two beat—John Sanders,

I think his name was. He had a day ticket. Do you remember him?"

"Yes, of course, the Canadian gentleman."

"That's him. Well, I was wondering if you'd mind if he took my place on the beats? He seems like a decent enough chap and he'd be company for Mr. Warburton."

"No problem at all, Mr. Powell. I seem to recall that he's staying at one of the local guesthouses. I can check our copy of the receipt for the address and try to get in touch with him, if you like."

"I'd be much obliged, Nigel."

"Not at all, Mr. Powell."

Powell stepped outside. As there was nearly half an hour until lunch, he decided on a stroll around the garden. Lost in thought, he rounded the corner of the hotel and nearly collided with Warburton and Arthur Ogden, who were returning from the river, rods in hand, engaged in an animated conversation.

"Well, speak of the devil," Warburton quipped.

"I was just going to tell Pinky about a rather curious incident that happened to me at the Old Bridge this morning, but he insisted that I should let you in on it as well," Ogden explained. He smiled thinly and ran his fingers through an impressive mane of white hair. Although nearly seventy, Ogden's rugged good looks seemed immune to the ravages of time. A self-educated man, he was at ease in any social circle and had tutored both princes and plumbers in the art of angling, as well as having written several authoritative books on the subject. "It's probably of no consequence whatsoever," he continued, "but perhaps Pinky's right. One never knows."

"I'm all ears," Powell said, his curiosity aroused.

"It was around nine o'clock," Ogden began. "I'd left my class to work on their casting and wandered up the river to see if I could catch a glimpse of a deer whose sign I'd come across earlier. I kept to the river path as far as the Old Bridge and then took to the hillside. I reckoned that the animal was bedded down in a thicket somewhere on the slope above the river. I was making my way through the scrub toward a rock outcropping, which looked like a good vantage point, when I nearly stepped on the bugger." He smiled sheepishly. "It's a good job I'm still continent, I can tell you. It was a young stag. He was off in a flash, leaving me shattered and feeling rather foolish.

"When my heart stopped pounding, I climbed onto the rock to see where he'd got to. I glassed the hillside, but there was no sign of him. Just as I was about to climb off, something caught my attention. There was a fisherman on the estate water. He was well upstream of the bridge around the first bend, which is why I hadn't spotted him from the river path. It seemed a bit rum, so I decided to investigate. Silly of me to stick my nose in, I suppose," he ventured tentatively.

Suppressing a surge of excitement, Powell smiled reassuringly. "Perfectly natural, Arthur. Do it all the time myself."

Apparently relieved to have escaped official admonishment for practicing detection without a license, Ogden continued in an increasingly animated fashion, "I picked my way along the slope, which had became unpleasantly steep and loose by this time, until I was at a point directly opposite and above him, perhaps fifty yards away. The chap had waded out into the river and was standing with his back to me, about ten yards from the near bank. He seemed completely unaware of my presence, my desperate scrabbling on the rocks above having no doubt been masked by the sound of the river." He paused, as if, in recalling the excitement of the moment, he needed to catch his breath.

"What did you do then?" prompted Warburton, who seemed to be taking considerable pleasure in the proceedings.

Ogden grinned sheepishly. "A damned foolish thing, now that I think of it. I'd come to the conclusion by then that I was dealing with a common poacher, and I'd just about made up my mind to challenge the fellow when I slipped on a patch of damp bracken. Somehow, I managed to grab on to something and arrest what might have been a rather spectacular descent, but in the process I dislodged a rock about the size of a football. I watched helplessly as the boulder bounded down the face and finally sailed in an apparently lethal trajectory toward my unwitting victim. I called out, but it was too late for him to react. The rock hit the water with a great commotion, missing him by mere inches. He let out a yelp and began to thrash his way back to shore, losing his rod in the process. One can hope that it was only river water that filled his waders." Ogden winked at Powell.

Warburton was shaking silently in near-apoplectic mirth while gesturing frantically for Ogden to continue.

"To cut a long story short, the poor bloke half swam, half crawled out of the water and, without so much as a glance over his shoulder, buggered off downstream like a scared rabbit."

"Interesting," Powell mused.

"And there's a rather curious footnote."

"What do you mean?"

"At that point I thought it best to leave well enough alone. I was about to start back when, all of a sudden, an unearthly wailing sound began to reverberate through the strath. It took me a few seconds to realize what it was." He looked incredulously at Powell. "It was someone playing the bloody bagpipes, if you can believe it! Difficult to say exactly where it was coming from, but it was damned eerie, I can tell you. Odd thing was, after a few minutes it stopped as suddenly as it had begun."

Powell's mind was racing. There was beginning to be too much clutter in this case for his liking. "Did you get a good look at him—the fisherman, I mean?"

Ogden shrugged. "Afraid not. I fancy I was shaking too much."

"Curious behavior for a poacher," Powell observed, as much to himself as anyone else.

"What do you mean?"

"Attempting to poach a salmon in broad daylight."

"Pretty brazen, I agree. Maybe he'd heard about the laird's demise and reckoned there'd be no one around to worry about it?"

"Perhaps." Powell considered this latest development. He'd better arrange for a diving team to attempt to recover the fishing rod. It was a slim chance, but worth a try. "Much obliged, Arthur. I think this may prove to be important."

Ogden grinned. "Always happy to help a copper."

"By the way, did you happen to notice the type of rod he was using?"

"What? Oh, the usual fourteen or fifteen footer. Why do you ask?"

"Are you certain?"

"Of course. I took particular notice because he wasn't very good with it."

Powell frowned. "That's a bit odd, don't you think?"

"What do you mean?"

"I don't know, I've always thought of poachers as being rather good at what they do."

Ogden shrugged. "Killing fish is the main thing—finesse is secondary. In fact, it's amazing how crude some of their methods can be. I recall a case where—"

"Gentlemen," Warburton interrupted heartily, consulting his watch, "unless I'm sadly mistaken, luncheon will be served shortly."

Feeling thoroughly sorry for himself, PC Shand had stopped in at Solway's for a cup of tea, although he'd been more in the mood for a few pints at the Grouse and Butt. In spite of his best efforts, he'd made painfully little progress in filling in the critical gap between the departure of Charles Murray and Oliver Pickens from Castle Glyn on Monday afternoon and the discovery of Murray's body in the River Spey the next day. He'd managed to ascertain that the two had stopped at a filling station in Grantown on Monday afternoon at approximately one-thirty, on the way to Aviemore presumably. Although neither man was known to the attendant, the lad had taken note of Murray's silver Mercedes and the Canadian accents. PC Shand chided himself; it wasn't much to show for four days of work.

As he stepped into the road he was faced with the immediate problem of what to do next. Rather than taking the High Street back to the police station, he turned down a narrow lane that ran parallel to the High Street behind various shops on the one side and a row of redbrick semis on the other. He always thought more clearly while walking, and here he could saunter along at his own pace; it wouldn't do to be seen by the public lounging about in the High Street. A few minutes later, having made precious little mental progress, he was approaching on his left an inconspicuous cleft between two buildings known as Leslie's Close, a narrow passage that led back through a tiny intervening courtyard to the High Street. As he was about to turn into the gap, he heard the soft murmur of voices, followed by a feminine sigh. He stopped, his curiosity aroused, and peered cautiously around the corner.

Less than twenty feet from where he stood was a couple locked in an amorous embrace. The man leaned against one wall with his back to Shand, partially screening the woman from view. Her arms were entwined around his neck. Impetuously unaware of the possibility of being observed, as lovers often are, they kissed passionately.

Being single in a small village and completely dedicated to his career, PC Shand had little opportunity or inclination for such diversions himself. Nevertheless, he was unable to avert his eyes, transfixed by a voyeuristic fascination mingled with embarrassment. His sense of duty soon intruded and he hurriedly weighed the courses of action open to him. Attempting to pass by in the intimate confines of the close was obviously out of the question. To his credit, he did not even consider the intrusively officious "What's all this, then?" Perhaps a discreet cough to announce his presence, followed by a decent interval to provide the couple with sufficient time to escape? Upon further reflection, he decided that it might be best under the circumstances to avoid the issue entirely by simply leaving the couple in peace and returning to the High Street the way he had come.

As he was preparing to tear himself away, the lovers shifted position slightly, presenting themselves to him in full profile. Recognition struck him like a thunderbolt.

CHAPTER 8

Powell drove abstractedly down the A95, his mind awhirl. He often felt a little overwhelmed at the point in an investigation where enough information was available to make things interesting, but no pattern had begun to emerge. In this case, however, even the most basic facts were few and far between. He inserted a cassette into the tape player and tapped his fingers on the steering wheel to the Pogues.

He went over it all again. Charles Murray, Canadian stock promoter and the new owner of Castle Glyn Estate, had been murdered last Monday night and fished from the River Spey some ten miles downstream of Kinlochy the next morning. Murray had last been seen alive in the company of one Oliver Pickens, another Canadian and a former business associate, on Monday afternoon en route to Aviemore, where Pickens, who had not been seen or heard from since, was thought to have boarded a train. And then there was the mystery fisherman whom Powell had seen on the estate water Monday evening only hours before Murray's murder, not to mention the inept poacher interrupted by Ogden in the same general vicinity this very morning. The possibility that they were one and the same person had not escaped him. And what about John Sanders, the Canadian tourist, who was surprisingly well informed about Murray and his affairs? Most troubling of all was the reaction of Ruby and the Whitelys whenever the subject of Charles Murray was raised. All things considered, Powell concluded uneasily, the elusive Mr. Pickens still remained the most interesting prospect.

There was little traffic on the motorway and Powell allowed his gaze to settle on the bare hills, pale amethyst and green, which rose abruptly ahead. High on a boulder-strewn slope he could make out a great tree bent and twisted into a fantastic bonsai by the elements: a relic of the ancient Caledonian pine forest and a monument to the stubborn persistence of nature in the face of civilization's onslaught. He squinted as if to etch the image in his mind. He felt a kind of kinship with the old tree.

It was in this cheery frame of mind that Powell crossed over the new Spey bridge at the picturesque village of Dulnay Bridge and turned off onto a narrow road that immediately doubled back upstream. Several miles and countless twists and turns later, he passed through the rusted wrought-iron gates of Castle Glyn. As he drove up the long drive that curved smoothly through a dense wood, he could not help thinking about the shareholders who had invested their hard-earned savings in one of Charles Murray's gold mines.

Castle Glyn, which had once encompassed some several thousand acres, had reached its zenith as a sporting estate before the Great War. Over the years its deer forests and grouse moors dotted with trout-filled lochs and miles of salmon fishing on the Spey had provided pleasant diversion for a succession of wealthy owners. After the war, however, the new economic realities had begun to intrude and the estate had fallen into a period of gradual decline. Although its fertile farmland still supplied barley to the local distilleries, most of the agricultural holdings had been sold off to the tenant farmers and, with the exception of the Spey fishing let to the Salar Lodge and a stretch upstream reserved for the laird, the sporting rights had been acquired by a London syndicate, which in turn had sold them on a time-share basis for an exorbitant profit.

For all that, the estate retained a modicum of its former glory and, after an initial twinge of disappointment at discovering that Castle Glyn was not in actual fact a castle, a visitor could hardly fail to be impressed by the first glimpse across rolling lawns. Its magnificent stone facade was well fenestrated in Georgian style, taking full advantage of a commanding view of the Spey Valley and the blue Highland hills beyond. The house was fronted by a rambling and overgrown garden of rhododendrons and giant azaleas, which one might fancifully suppose was a colorful moat to deter rival clans.

Powell parked his car, mounted the broad stone steps, and rang the bell. While he waited, he took in his surroundings—the cracked masonry and sprouting weeds. Sign of the times, he supposed. Eventually the door swung open, revealing an ancient and decrepit butler. Ross, presumably.

"Good afternoon. I'm Chief Superintendent Powell. I believe Miss Murray is expecting me."

"Please follow me, sir," the butler croaked.

Powell was shown to a large room that had obviously served as Murray's study.

"I will inform Miss Murray, sir." And with that, Ross tottered precariously out.

Powell examined the room with interest. He took it as axiomatic that the things with which people chose to surround themselves revealed much about their personalities. The high walls in dark oak paneling were hung with the usual stags' heads and sporting prints, and dominating the room along the right wall was a massive stone hearth, above which was mounted a very large salmon. Remnants of the previous laird's tenure, he surmised.

On either side of the hearth, tall shelves overflowed with old books and on the wall opposite stood a magnificent French walnut cabinet, which revealed through leaded glass doors a collection of shotguns and rifles. The parquet floor was covered with a slightly tatty Persian carpet and in the center of the room stood a large mahogany writing table surrounded by three well-worn smoking chairs. Powell noticed that there were a few scraps of feather, tinsel, and other fly-tying paraphernalia scattered across the table's cracked leather top. At the rear of the study a French window opened to a large flagstone courtyard, in the center of which stood a rusty fountain, now dry, which represented, Powell fancied, some sort of mythical spouting beast.

He turned his attention back to the room. A little grandiose for his taste, but there was no denying that the place possessed a comfortable, lived-in sort of ambience. As he was perusing the titles in the bookcase, mostly country life and nature subjects, he heard the door open.

"Mr. Powell, I presume."

Powell turned and was presented with a young woman whose singular beauty left him momentarily speechless.

"I'm sorry I kept you waiting." She smiled, making any reply superfluous.

"Ah, yes, well, thank you for agreeing to see me on such short notice, Miss Murray," he said quickly. "This must be a difficult time for you."

"Yes, it is." She regarded him with apparent interest and then turned and walked across the room to the writing table.

To his acute embarrassment, Powell found himself having unchaste thoughts. He would have been hard pressed, however, to put into words exactly what it was about the young woman that he found so attractive. Her ginger hair was cut short, making her seem taller than she was, and she had striking green eyes that seemed both expressive and somehow unfathomable at the same time. Even the plain wool skirt and loose Fair Isle jumper she wore seemed inexplicably provocative. Powell concluded that Heather Murray's appeal was uncontrived and more an expression of her personality than of any particular physical attribute.

Reluctantly bringing his mind back to the business at hand, he composed his thoughts as he waited for her to sit down. At her invitation he selected a chair opposite. He tried not to think about it as she crossed her legs.

"Miss Murray, as I explained to you on the telephone, I am assisting the Scottish authorities with their inquiry into your father's death. Information has recently come to light suggesting that foul play may have been involved and, while I realize that it may be difficult for you, I'm afraid I have to ask you some questions."

"I understand, of course; it's a policeman's job to be difficult, isn't it?" Her eyes sparkled.

"We endeavor, Miss Murray, to inconvenience only the criminal element," Powell rejoined, beginning to feel more at ease.

Suddenly her expression, without seeming to change outwardly, was serious. Powell decided that it had something to do with her eyes.

"You must know that I've already spoken to your Mr. Barrett."

"Yes. But if you'll bear with me, I'd like to cover some of the same ground again. I'm a bit of a plodder, you see."

She looked skeptical. "You don't look like a plodder to me, Mr. Powell."

He coughed. "Yes—well—now, Miss Murray, I understand that your father was involved in the mining industry back in Canada. Perhaps you could begin by telling me something about his work?"

She did not reply immediately and Powell got the distinct impression that she was in some way evaluating him.

"My father was a geologist by training," she began in an even voice. "After the war he worked for several large Canadian and American mining firms in the mineral exploration field. Eventually he struck out on his own with a small exploration company. In the late seventies he staked a number of claims at Ptarmigan Mountain near the Alaskan panhandle in northwestern British Columbia. He sank everything he had into the venture. It was mostly moose pasture, as he was fond of saying later, and the initial drilling results were not very promising. But my father was a stubborn man and he somehow managed to raise enough money to continue the exploration work. There were numerous disappointments and setbacks, but he persevered and eventually discovered a large gold deposit."

She smiled faintly. "It was a real family affair in those days. My mother cooked for the men in the drilling camps. I remember her telling the most harrowing stories of life in the bush, fending off giant mosquitoes and grizzly bears. It may seem hard to believe now, but I was born in a log cabin surrounded by glaciers. They had to fly the doctor in by helicopter."

Powell grinned. "With a background like that, we Brits must seem a boring lot." He paused to give her an opportunity to dispute this suggestion, of which she chose not to avail herself. He cleared his throat. "Ah, please continue, Miss Murray."

"There's not much more to tell, really. My mother died when I was ten and my father never really got over it. I think he compensated by putting even more time and energy into his business, until his retirement two years ago."

Powell had listened to Heather Murray with growing interest. He had come to Castle Glyn with a notion of Charles Murray as a rather questionable character, a man with a checkered past at the very least, but he had just been given a glimpse of someone more complex, someone he could perhaps begin to understand. Still, she had not told him what he really wanted to know.

"Miss Murray, I'm curious about the financial side of your father's business—how he raised the necessary capital to carry on his exploration work, for instance."

"I was wondering when you'd get around to that," she said matter-of-factly. She explained patiently, giving the impression that she'd done it many times before, "Mineral exploration is a very risky and expensive business, Mr. Powell. Basically, you have to find a way to finance the work with no guarantee of any return. Funds are normally raised by offering shares to the public or to private individuals and, obviously, prospective investors need to be convinced that they stand a reasonable chance of making a profit. Money and hope, Mr. Powell, are the twin currencies of the mining business. That's where the promotion comes in. You need to sell the story and downplay the risks. Nine times out of ten you'll miss the mark completely, and even when you find something, the reality is that very few properties will ever support economically viable mines. So there is no doubt that the majority of investors in small exploration companies will lose money in the long run. On the other hand, if one is astute and not too greedy, the profits can be enormous. A little luck doesn't hurt either."

She regarded him steadily. "Please don't misunderstand me, Mr. Powell. I am not naive. But I refuse to believe that my father was dishonest, if that's what you're wondering about."

"I have no reason to doubt you, Miss Murray, but given the nature of the business, wouldn't it be fair to assume that he might have made some enemies along the way?"

She appeared to consider this suggestion carefully. "I suppose it depends upon what you mean, exactly, by enemies."

"People who lost money investing in his various projects, for instance."

"Like fish in the sea."

"Miss Murray," Powell said patiently, "I understand from Mr. Barrett that your father had been the target of various threats over the years. Now, I want you to think about this very carefully. Do you know of anyone in particular who might have had a score to settle with him?"

"No one with sufficient reason to murder him, if that's what you mean. Look, Mr. Powell, the majority of people who invest in the sort of companies my father promoted are basically looking to make a fast buck. Some undoubtedly underestimate the risks involved, others are simply greedy. Either way, when they make money they crow about how smart they are; when they lose they bitch about it. It's human nature."

"That's a bit cynical, isn't it?"

She laughed unaffectedly like a schoolgirl. "That's an interesting observation, coming from a policeman."

Powell smiled. "Touché." Their eyes met, and he had to make a conscious effort to continue. "Miss Murray, I understand that you called Ruby MacGregor at the Salar Lodge on Tuesday morning."

"Yes."

"Do you mind telling me why?"

She hesitated. "I told Mr. Barrett that I'd spent the weekend with a friend in Pitlochry. I neglected to mention that I'd quarreled with my father before I left. I was still upset about it when I got back Monday night. I'd hoped to speak to him, but he wasn't here—I mean he . . ." She seemed unable to continue.

"What time did you arrive home?" Powell prompted gently.

"Around ten-thirty, I think."

"What did you do when you realized that your father was out?"

"I was tired, so I went to bed. When I discovered the next morning that he still hadn't returned, I was beside myself. So I called Ruby—to see if he'd been at the Salar Lodge."

"Why did you think that he might have gone to the hotel?"

"I—I don't know really. It was just a feeling."

"Did he go there often?"

"No, not often."

Powell searched her face. "What about Monday night in particular? Can you think of any reason he might have gone to the Salar Lodge? For a drink, perhaps?"

"My father didn't drink," she replied sharply.

"Miss Murray, the results of the postmortem indicate that your father had sufficient alcohol in his blood to render him intoxicated at the time of his death."

She suddenly looked very pale. She sighed and brushed a strand of hair from her forehead. "If only I'd . . ."

Powell gave her the opportunity to elaborate and when she did not, he said quietly, "Would you like to tell me about it?"

She spoke mechanically. "My father used to be a hard drinker. I've spent half my life trying to hide it—from my friends, from myself. It went with the sort of life he led, I guess, but after he retired it became almost unbearable. Then one day he found some pot in my room. There was the inevitable blowup, as you can imagine, but in the end I think it brought us closer together. He promised me then that he'd give up drinking and he was true to his word."

"I see. Can you tell me what you and your father quarreled about?"

"I'd rather not. It's personal, but I can assure you it has nothing to do with what happened."

"That seems fairly definite."

"It is."

Time to change gears. "I take it you know this Oliver Pickens?"

"Yes. He is—he was a business associate of my father's from the old days. I hadn't heard Father talk about him for years."

"Were you aware that Mr. Pickens was spending the weekend at Castle Glyn?"

"No, Father didn't mention it."

"Do you suppose Pickens might have just dropped in out of the blue?"

"It's possible, I suppose," she said doubtfully.

"It may be important, Miss Murray. Would you mind if I questioned the staff about it?"

"No, of course not. But I'm not sure I understand . . ."

"If one were planning a murder, it's unlikely that one would openly arrange to be the intended victim's only house guest at the time."

"Yes—yes, I see."

"Were you personally acquainted with Pickens?"

"I met him years ago, but I'm not sure I'd even recognize him now."

"Do you know if he might have had some business to conduct with your father?"

"My father didn't confide in me about his business affairs, but I suppose it's possible. I know he still kept his hand in to some extent."

"Do you know if Pickens might have borne some grudge against your father?"

She shook her head. "No, I'm sorry."

Powell swore silently. He had been hoping for more. "Miss Murray, I must admit to being a bit curious about your father's reasons for coming to Kinlochy."

She shrugged lightly. "I don't think he ever really planned to retire, but he had some sort of disagreement with the other directors of the company he was promoting at the time, and they tried to force him out. Father had the support of the shareholders, so there's no doubt he could have stayed on if he'd wanted to, but I think he'd just had enough. He resigned from the boards of all of his companies, although he remained a major shareholder in several of them. He was quite bitter about it, but eventually I think he realized that he needed to put it all behind him and get on with his life. He'd spent quite a lot of time in the UK over the years and had fallen in love with Scotland. He often said that the Highlands reminded him of home." She toyed absently with a small feather. "My paternal grandfather was a Scot and, at the risk of sounding trite, I think he felt some sort of connection with his ancestral homeland, although I'm sure he would never have put it that way. Anyway, he'd heard about Castle Glyn from a business associate and a few months later we moved in." She paused thoughtfully. "Also, I think there were too many memories associated with my mother back home."

"And what about you, Miss Murray?"

"What about me, Mr. Powell?" She looked at him with those penetrating green eyes.

"You're obviously an independent young woman. No doubt you had friends and a life of your own in Canada. You must have had to pull up roots to come here."

Her eyes flashed. "I thought my father needed me. Is that so difficult to understand? Besides, I don't see that it's any of your business."

Powell felt strangely wounded. "Please forgive me, Miss Murray; it is not my intention to pry into your personal affairs. I can assure you that my only concern is to find out what happened to your father." But even as he spoke, he felt like a pompous arse.

Heather Murray sat motionless. Eventually she said quietly, "I'm sorry. It's just that right from the beginning it was obvious we didn't belong here. But there was nothing left for Father back home, and with so much time on his hands . . ." She hesitated. "Mr. Powell, my father wasn't perfect, not by a long shot, and we didn't always agree on things, but I know he had my best interests at heart." Her voice trembled slightly. "Please forgive me— I suppose the strain is beginning to take its toll."

"I understand." There was a difficult moment as he considered the inevitability of his next question. "Miss Murray, you've hinted that your father was not entirely happy at Castle Glyn. Is it possible that he became depressed and took his own life?"

Her eyes were unwavering. "Suicide is out of the question, Mr. Powell. You didn't know my father. He would never have taken the easy way out."

Powell nodded, satisfied. "Just one more question, Miss Murray: Did you happen to notice whether your father's car was here when you got home Monday night? I understand it was found parked in its usual place in the garage Tuesday morning."

She shook her head. "I didn't think to check. I suppose I just assumed he'd taken it."

"Thank you, Miss Murray. You've been most helpful. I promise to let you know the moment there is anything to report." He stood up. An awkward pause. "Do you need any help with the arrangements?"

"I'm managing all right, thanks. I've got a few more things to clear up here and then I'll be going home."

"I see. Well, let me know if there's anything I can do. Anything at all."

"Yes, of course." He knew somehow that she wouldn't be calling him.

"Fine. I'll let myself out."

She smiled without conviction. "Goodbye, Mr. Powell."

He could sense her eyes on his back as he left the room.

Before leaving Castle Glyn, he managed to track down Ross. "Did Mr. Murray give any indication before he left with Mr. Pickens on Monday afternoon that he was expecting another guest?"

Ross thought strenuously for what seemed an interminable time. "Not exactly, sir," he wheezed eventually. "However, he did make a remark about the silver, sir."

"What?"

"He told me to polish the silver, sir."

"And what do you make of that?"

Ross cocked his head. "I beg your pardon, sir?"

Powell repeated the question with exaggerated precision.

"Well, sir, it was his way of telling me that he wanted everything shipshape, in a manner of speaking, sir."

"I see. And you're certain he didn't mention anything about another visitor?"

"Not that I can recall, sir."

"Just one more thing, Ross. Would you say that Mr. Pickens's visit was an amicable one?"

Ross looked puzzled.

"I mean," Powell said loudly, "did he and Mr. Murray have words or anything like that?"

The butler drew himself up to full height, or would have had he been able, and sniffed, whether as a result of indignation or a sinus condition Powell was unable to determine. "I'm sure I really couldn't say, sir."

"Thank you, Ross. That will be all." He made a mental note to have Shand interview the other domestics.

When he got back to the Salar Lodge, there was word waiting from Barrett. They had located Oliver Pickens.

CHAPTER 9

Powell stared out the window of his darkened sleeper as the coach rocked and swayed through the impenetrable blackness. The first blush of dawn was still an hour away and occasionally he could see the lights of a cottage or farmhouse in the distance, with curtained windows that were cosily inviting yet nostalgically remote and unattainable. He switched on the reading light and noticed his wan reflection in the window. Not yet fifty, with most of his hair and just enough gray to look experienced, he was supposedly in his prime. But at that moment he felt bloody old.

When Barrett had suggested that he return to London to interview Oliver Pickens, he had jumped at the chance. He knew that he needed to get away from Kinlochy for a while, as if by physically removing himself from the scene he might regain a sense of perspective. He had been in the midst of packing when Shand arrived at the Salar Lodge and dropped his bombshell about Heather Murray and young Whitely. The revelation weighed heavily on him and he had been unable to sleep since boarding the train at Aviemore. He knew he was reacting like an adolescent fool, but the young woman had stirred something in him that he hadn't felt for a long time. The sensation was unsettling.

He turned to his book and began to read in a desultory fashion but found himself unable to concentrate. He tossed the book aside and turned off the light. Eventually, lulled by the hypnotic clattering of the train, he slipped fitfully into the embrace of a faceless succubus.

The train pulled into Euston Station shortly before eight A.M. It was a typical damp, gray London morning. Powell hailed a taxi and arrived home as the breakfast dishes were being cleared. He detected the lingering aroma of bacon and coffee.

A few minutes later over a disappointing oat bran muffin (Marion insisted that it was just the thing for his cholesterol), he was explaining his surprise appearance. "I was going to call last night, but it was late and I didn't want to wake you." Was that the real reason? he wondered. "There's been a break in the case; we've located a key witness in London and I've come down to interview him. If all goes well, I'll be returning to Scotland tomorrow night."

Marion frowned slightly. "I wish I'd known. We might have done something tonight, but I've made arrangements to take the boys up to Ely to visit Sarah. We won't be getting back until late tomorrow, so I probably won't see you."

Powell had forgotten that it was Spring Bank holiday. "I wouldn't want you to change your plans on my account. You don't see your sister that often."

"No, I suppose not."

There was a lengthy silence.

"How are things—in Scotland, I mean?"

"All right."

"Not much of a holiday, I take it."

"You know how it is."

"Duty calls." She gave a mock salute.

"Something like that."

She placed her hand on his arm. "You should really try to unwind, Ers. Life's too short."

"You're telling me."

"I know things have been getting you down lately. But all you seem to think about is work." She brushed the hair from her face, exasperated. "For goodness' sake, you're supposed to be on holiday."

"Since when have you been so interested in my so-called holiday?"

"Look, I understand you need to get away, not that it seems to do you any good."

"You'd be surprised."

"I'm serious, Ers."

"So am I."

"I think we need to spend more time together."

He shrugged. "It's hard to find the time, isn't it?" He searched her face carefully. "What's this all about, if you don't mind me asking?"

"I've just been thinking, that's all."

"A dangerous pastime, in my experience." He rose abruptly from the table. "Where are the boys?"

She sighed. "Upstairs, I imagine."

For the first time, he felt, rather than heard, the faint thump of music. "I'll go see."

Later, after Peter and David had gone off to a football match, he and Marion made love. It was spontaneous, unexpected. All the more so since he would have been hard pressed to recall when they'd last slept together. It had begun innocently enough, Marion brushing against him as they passed in the upstairs hallway. Her breast touching his arm and the scent of her hair. She had turned to say something, reaching for him as his mouth silenced hers.

Afterward, as she lay contentedly in his arms, she interpreted his silence as the unspoken ease of long familiarity. In reality he was feeling slightly guilty; he'd been thinking about Heather Murray.

When Powell arrived at the Yard he found Detective-Sergeant Bill Black on the early turn.

"How's the holiday, Mr. Powell?" Black remarked affably with a barely suppressed chortle.

"Very funny. Anything for me?"

"A fax from Inverness this morning. It's on your desk."

Powell grunted. "How's our friend?"

"He's cooling his heels downstairs, and I'm given to understand that he's not very happy about it."

"Have him brought up to one of the interview rooms."

"Right."

"Say, was I seeing things, or did I see a copy of *The Collected Poems of John Donne* on your desk?" Powell called out to the sergeant.

"It's for an evening class, sir."

Powell examined his colleague with interest. "Really?"

Sergeant Black looked slightly embarrassed as he nodded and turned to go downstairs.

Powell poured a cup of coffee and spent the next fifteen minutes reviewing the material Barrett had sent. Occasionally he pursed his lips in a silent whistle.

The interview room was sparsely furnished with a Formica table bolted to the floor and two molded plastic chairs that were intended to bounce harmlessly off the cranium if thrown by a dissatisfied client. There were no windows, but special fluorescent lighting, prescribed by psychologists to soothe the savage breast, created a warm pink ambience that Powell found mildly irritating. None of your naked swinging light bulbs and rubber hosepipes these days, as Detective-Sergeant Black had once been heard to remark a trifle wistfully.

Oliver Pickens was already seated at the table. Without a word, Powell sat down across from him. Detective-Sergeant Black stood unobtrusively in the corner, slightly behind and to the right of Pickens, notebook at the ready.

Pickens was not at all as Powell had imagined him. Pinched and slightly astringent in appearance, with wire-rimmed spectacles and sartorial tastes tending toward the funereal, he did not fit Powell's mental image of a red-blooded stock promoter. More like the common variety of ferret you'd find in a Soho porn shop.

Pickens stared inimically at Powell. "What the hell's this all about?" he demanded in a sharp, unpleasantly nasal voice. "Why have I been arrested?"

Powell began easily, "First things first, Mr. Pickens. I'm Chief Superintendent Powell and this is Detective-Sergeant Black. Now, to answer your question, you have not been arrested. You have been asked to voluntarily attend here because we are hoping that you'll be able to assist us with our inquiry into the murder of Charles Murray, who, I believe, was an acquaintance of yours."

"What choice do I have?" Pickens whined.

"You are, of course, free to leave at any time. We simply wish to ask you a few questions."

"Like I told the sergeant, I found out about Charlie only when I read about it in the papers."

"Oh, yes?" Powell yawned. "Now, Mr. Pickens, let's not beat about the bush. I understand that you were Mr. Murray's guest at Castle Glyn last weekend. What was the purpose of your visit?"

"It's none of your goddamn business."

Powell sighed inwardly. He could see that it was going to be one of those days.

"Sergeant Black, I don't think Mr. Pickens fully appreciates the situation." He got up and walked around the table behind Pickens and began to pace back and forth.

"Are you trying to intimidate me?" Pickens demanded, twisting awkwardly in his chair to face Powell.

"Not at all, Mr. Pickens. I'm just trying to figure out what your game is and what you could possibly hope to gain by being uncooperative. Perhaps you're just a bit thick."

Pickens did not reply. A tiny muscle below his right eye had begun to twitch spasmodically.

Powell returned to his chair and considered his options. Better to be safe than sorry, he decided. "Last Monday night," he continued equably, "between eight o'clock and midnight, someone bashed Charles Murray on the head and then chucked him into the River Spey. We know that you were with Murray, and we have every reason to believe that you were the last person to see him alive. Up to this point, I've considered you to be a potential witness, not necessarily a suspect, but I'm afraid I'm beginning to have second thoughts."

Realization seemed to dawn on Pickens and his facial tic became even more pronounced.

Powell stood up and walked to the door. "Sergeant Black."

Black followed him out, locking the door behind them.

"Read him his rights. I'm going upstairs to brief Merriman."

"Yes, sir."

Powell returned about fifteen minutes later. "Sergeant Black has already cautioned you, but I'm going to ask you again: Do you wish to contact a solicitor?"

"I don't need a goddamn lawyer—I haven't done anything wrong!"

"That's as may be, but I must remind you that we suspect your involvement in the murder of Charles Murray. Do you understand?"

"I'm not an idiot and I—" He checked himself. One could almost hear the wheels turning. He seemed to come to a decision and began to speak rapidly, "See here, I have an important business engagement on Tuesday and I can't afford any, er, inconvenience, so let's get this over with. Ask me any questions you like."

"Much better, Mr. Pickens. We're particularly interested in your whereabouts from the time you were seen leaving Castle Glyn with Mr. Murray on Monday to your arrival in London."

"It's true that I spent last weekend with Charlie Murray,

but I can assure you that he was alive and kicking when he put me on the train at Aviemore. That was the last time I saw him."

"What time did you leave Castle Glyn?"

"I don't remember exactly—sometime after lunch. Charlie's butler can vouch for that. The Edinburgh train leaves Aviemore around three-thirty and I wanted to get there in plenty of time."

"So you boarded a train at Aviemore on Monday afternoon—what did you say your destination was?"

"Edinburgh, I just told you."

So much for any pretense of civility. "Ah, yes, of course. Tell me, Mr. Pickens, what did you do in Edinburgh? A little shopping in Princes Street, perhaps?"

Pickens grinned slyly. "As a matter of fact, I decided on the spur of the moment to continue on to York."

"Really. Why was that?"

"I changed my mind. It's a free country, isn't it?"

"All right. What did you do in York?"

"Nothing much, as it turned out. I was so beat that I slept right through and didn't wake up until the train got into London around midnight. As the last train north had just left, I spent the rest of the night in London. Seeing the sights, you might say." He leered unpleasantly. "The next morning I caught the first train back to York."

"A rather convoluted itinerary, I'd say. Is there anyone who can corroborate your story?"

Pickens shrugged.

"Nobody saw you? You spoke to no one?"

"Even if there was someone, a gentleman shouldn't kiss and tell, should he?" Smirk.

The prospect of Oliver Pickens kissing anything didn't

bear thinking about. But for the time being, Powell thought, he could worry about his own alibi.

"Tell me, why were you so anxious to get to York?"

"Because it's in Yorkshire," Pickens replied with contrived innocence.

"I'll bite. Why Yorkshire?"

"Let's just say I'm a big fan of James Herriot." Snigger.

Powell did his best to conjure up a mental image of the venerable vet with his arm buried to the shoulder up a certain bespectacled horse's arse. He smiled benignly. "I assume that you eventually arrived at your destination. Then what?"

"I hired a car and spent a couple of days touring the Dales."

"That covers a lot of territory. Can you be a little more specific?"

"Wensleydale and Swaledale, if you must know."

"Very scenic."

"I was particularly interested in the local geology. The Buttertubs, for example, were very impressive."

"I take your point, Mr. Pickens. You can rest assured that we will be checking your story in every detail. Now, you returned to London, suitably refreshed, I presume, from your sojourn amongst the high fells—when?"

Pickens's eyes narrowed. "Friday night. You know the rest. By the way, I don't much care for your attitude. I may just have to speak to your superiors."

"My superiors are well aware of my attitude, believe me. Now, when did you say you first learned about Charles Murray's death?"

Pickens began picking his teeth. "I don't remember

exactly. I picked up a newspaper someplace and saw the story buried in the back pages."

"Then you'd have read the other bit about the police being eager to interview a Canadian tourist, one Oliver Pickens, in the hope that he might be able to assist them with their inquiries."

"Gee, I must have missed that part. You see, I'm not much interested in current affairs. Too depressing."

God, this is bloody tedious, Powell thought. His head had begun to pound. "I should tell you while you're formulating your next flippancy that I'm thinking about adjourning our little chat to give you time to consider your position. In the meantime we can offer you a night of commodious accommodation compliments of Her Majesty. Whether or not you choose to avail yourself is entirely up to you."

In the corner, Detective-Sergeant Black was grinning like a large ape.

"I know my rights," Pickens whined. "You can't hold me without grounds. Look, I've answered all your questions. What more do you want?"

Powell regarded him with barely concealed distaste. Pickens was cringing now like a beaten dog, but not the type you would want to turn your back on. "To be precise, Mr. Pickens, we can detain you for up to twenty-four hours while we decide what to do with you." He had made up his mind. "Why don't we take a break while you think it over." He motioned to Black, and before Pickens could protest they had stepped out of the room.

"Nasty piece of work, that," Detective-Sergeant Black remarked pleasantly.

Powell grimaced. "Let him stew for a while and then take a formal statement. While you're at it, try to extract a bit more detail on his comings and goings. Then lock him up and get started on his story."

"Right."

"I get the distinct impression he's a bit skittish about his so-called business appointment on Tuesday. We'll have to play that up for all its worth. I'm afraid if we can't get our teeth into something more substantial, we'll have to let him go. At least for the time being."

"His story seems plausible," Black rumbled.

"We'll know soon enough."

Powell returned to his office and sent out for a sandwich. He spent the remainder of the afternoon in bureaucratic fettle, clearing off his desk. At five o'clock he left New Scotland Yard and walked briskly in a fine drizzle to the tube station at St. James' Park. Except for a few damp sightseers, the streets seemed oddly deserted. He changed at Embankment Station, continuing on foot from Goodge Street to his destination.

It had begun to pour, the rain slanting like tinsel against the black buildings. Just ahead he could see a faded green awning under a jagged blue neon signscape that was intended, he supposed, to represent the high Himalayas but which looked in the thickening mist more like the surreal brain wave trace of some deranged acidhead. Powell collapsed his umbrella under the dripping awning and entered the fragrant and enveloping warmth of the K2 Tandoori Restaurant.

He inhaled deeply. The atmosphere was redolent with

the complex aromas of fenugreek, cloves, cinnamon, and coriander. He was greeted almost instantaneously by the proprietor, a small ebullient Pakistani named Rashid Jamal. "My dear Erskine, this is indeed an unexpected pleasure! Here, let me take your coat. I thought you were in Scotland pursuing the salmon?"

Powell smiled. "I had to return to London on business for a couple of days, Rashid. Marion's away for the weekend and I couldn't face the prospect of cold pie at home, so here I am."

His host beamed. "I am absolutely delighted," he said, gesturing toward Powell's usual table near the window.

"I desperately need a pint of something soothing, Rashid. Will you join me?"

"It would be my pleasure, Erskine!"

While his host repaired to the bar, Powell surveyed his familiar surroundings amidst the muted strains of a recorded sitar and tabla. The dining area of the K2 was arranged in a horseshoe-shaped configuration, with the bar and general service area situated in the center. At the rear of the restaurant, which corresponded to the open end of the horseshoe, access to the kitchen was obtained by way of swinging doors, through which on a busy night one could get tantalizing glimpses of frenetic culinary activity. From his vantage point at the front of the restaurant, Powell could see that he was the only customer. It was still early, however, and he savored the solitude. The red flock walls were decorated with assorted prints and batiks depicting lavishly bejeweled sultans and maharanis in various erotic but highly improbable positions. And, as always, the bar was festively, if unseasonably, festooned with strings of red-and-green Christmas lights.

Rashid soon returned with a pint of bitter for Powell and a tonic and lime for himself.

Powell raised his glass. "Cheers, Rashid." He took a grateful gulp. How are Nindi and the kids?"

"Fine, fine. And your family?"

"Keeping me hopping."

"Good, good."

Powell couldn't resist the opportunity. "I see another Balti house has opened down the street."

Rashid's eyes flashed angrily. "Balti-shmalti! I have been cooking fresh food in the karahi for twenty years, but I refuse to cater to lager louts!"

"Thank God for that," Powell replied. He took another long draft of his beer and then sighed heavily. "Tell me, Rashid, do you think I could make a go of it in the curry restaurant business?"

Rashid grinned. "Oh, undoubtedly, Erskine, undoubtedly. But I am not at all certain that I would like the competition." He examined his companion closely and then frowned, evincing an air of deep concern. "But why would you ask such a question?"

"They say a change is as good as a rest."

"What are you saying, my friend? Yours is an honorable profession. There is no higher calling than to labor for the public good."

Powell shrugged. "I don't know, Rashid. Marion says it's male menopause. And an inability to get in touch with my feelings, no bloody doubt." He grimaced and took another sip of his beer.

Rashid nodded sadly in a gesture of masculine commiseration. "I know what you mean, my friend, but think

how terrible it would be if there were no honest policemen like yourself to protect the innocent citizenry like
myself," he said earnestly.

Powell managed a thin smile. "I do appreciate the sen-
timent, Rashid, honestly. But what about you? Have you
ever regretted not becoming a doctor like your father?"

Rashid laughed infectiously. "I learned long ago that the
key to health and long life is a happy tummy, and I have
steadfastly devoted my life to that principle ever since. But
seriously, my friend," he persisted, "the grass frequently
appears greener on the other side of the mountain range.
As my dear old mother used to say—or perhaps it was
Tom Jones, I cannot remember now—enlightenment is
frequently to be found under one's very nose. You know,
the green, green grass of home. Hee hee!" His dark eyes
twinkled. "My mother used to say also that we are all just
gravy spots on the tablecloth of life. But remember, Erskine,
my dear chap, spicy fellows like you and I are damn difficult to wash out, yes?"

Powell grinned in spite of himself. "Your mother was
a very wise woman, Rashid."

"Now, enough philosophy—you must be famished.
May I order your usual on the house tonight for this special occasion?"

"Rashid, I couldn't, really," Powell protested.

"But, Erskine, I insist."

Powell thought quickly. "Look, I've got a freshly
smoked salmon at home. I'll bring it for you tomorrow."
As he spoke, he couldn't help wondering what Marion
would think of the arrangement.

Rashid gravely pondered the proposition for a moment
and then grinned. "Done!"

As he tucked in to his meal Powell noticed that Rashid had replaced the Indian music tape with Tom Jones: "The Green, Green Grass of Home" was playing.

CHAPTER 10

At eight-thirty the next morning, one week after Charles Murray's murder, Powell sat in his office at New Scotland Yard with Detective-Sergeant Black.

"Well, Bill, let's have it."

Black drew out his notebook and placed it carefully on the desk in front of him, as if for easy reference. But in all the years they had worked together Powell had never seen him once refer to it after his customary note-taking.

"I've had a chance to check most of the particulars," Black began, "but I'm afraid the results are not entirely satisfactory, sir."

"They seldom are. Go on."

"It seems that Pickens did indeed stay at a hotel in York, the Park Royal, on Tuesday night. According to the clerk on duty at the time, a gentleman fitting the general description of our chap checked in at approximately two-thirty Tuesday afternoon. He wasn't seen until the next morning, having fully recovered apparently from the rigors of his evening in London." Black paused, as if to allow his superior an opportunity to comment. When there was no response he continued, "He hired a car from the local Avis agency and drove north to Richmond, where he put up for the night at a guesthouse called the Drover's Rest. The next day—that would be Thursday— he drove up Swaledale, then took the hill road from Muker over the pass into Wensleydale. He spent the night in Hawes at a bed-and-breakfast establishment. Then back to York on Friday to drop off the car and on to London by train that evening. His credit card receipts for lodging and petrol check out, by the way. All in all, sir," Black concluded comfortably, "not an unusual itinerary for your average tourist."

"Perhaps. But I'm still interested in the gap between the time he left Kinlochy with Murray and his arrival in York."

"I've checked with the Scottish lads this morning, sir. Nothing new there, I'm afraid."

Powell considered the problem aloud. "The pathologist has fixed the time of death at around midnight or a little before. If that's true, our man couldn't have done it, assuming that he was in fact on that train to Edinburgh. Alternatively, he could have hung about Kinlochy until Tuesday morning. Which would have taken a fair bit of nerve if he'd just committed a murder, don't you think? Or possibly he had a car?" Powell looked at Detective-Sergeant Black.

Black shrugged.

"Let's get on with it," Powell said.

Oliver Pickens seemed somewhat subdued after a night in the nick. He looked up furtively as Powell and Black entered the room.

"Well, Mr. Pickens, have you thought it over?" Powell asked brusquely.

Pickens blinked his bleary eyes. "Look, I promise you, I did not kill Charles Murray. He was a pal of mine, for God's sake! I'll help you any way I can. I just want to get this thing over with. I have my reputation to consider." He seemed to be making a concerted effort to modulate his usual nasal whine.

"Let's discuss that last little item," Powell replied cheerily, not at all convinced by this apparent change of heart. He consulted the docket he had brought with him. "I am informed that you were formerly the president of a now defunct mining company called Golden Fleece Resources Limited, which was listed on the Vancouver Stock Exchange from eighty-one to eighty-four. Is that correct?"

Pickens fidgeted. "Yeah, what of it?"

"I understand further that as a result of certain, shall we say, irregularities trading in the stock of this company was suspended by the regulatory authorities in July of eighty-four."

"They never proved a thing." Pickens's whine had started up again like a jet turbine.

"I believe the particular allegation was insider trading, which as I understand the term—and correct me if I'm wrong—means profiting illegally from information not available to the investing public at large. My sources also indicate that, while formal charges were never laid in the case, your trading privileges on the VSE were suspended for three years. Is that also true?"

"I have nothing more to say," Pickens said sulkily.

"As you wish. But not to put too fine a point on it, Mr.

Pickens, it seems that reputation of yours is already a bit tarnished."

Pickens sprang to his feet with sudden vehemence. "I won't sit here and be insulted," he keened. "I'm no fool. You have absolutely nothing on me. It's all a bluff and I'll not stand for it another minute."

Powell regarded him placidly. "When you're quite finished you can sit down again. You won't be going anywhere until we're done with you, so you might as well relax." Better not push too hard.

Sullenly acquiescent, Pickens collapsed into his chair.

"Yesterday you alluded to a certain business engagement tomorrow. Would you like to tell me about it?"

"That's my affair—it has nothing to do with what happened to Charlie."

"Perhaps not, but I would suggest that it has everything to do with your visit to Castle Glyn."

Pickens turned deathly pale. "What do you know about it?"

"I know that the reason you're in the UK is to promote your latest venture—" Powell grimaced "—Lucky Diamond Mining Corporation, to be specific. And the reason you went to see Charles Murray was to call in an old debt." Powell paused to let this suggestion sink in.

Pickens seemed unable to reply. His eye muscles twitched like the spasms of a fatally stricken bird.

"When Charles Murray began exploration work on his mining claims in northern British Columbia," Powell continued, "he needed a promoter to help him raise the necessary capital, and you, Mr. Pickens, were the very man. As a result of your undoubted talents in that line, and a bit of luck on Murray's part, the venture succeeded beyond anyone's wildest dreams. Unfortunately for you, due to bad luck or bad timing, you did not profit from the subsequent spectacular rise in the company's share price—"

"That's because the son of a bitch screwed me," Pickens hissed. "The initial assay results weren't any good, so when Charlie offered to take my stock off me, like he was doing me a favor, I took him up on it. A few weeks later," he continued in a shrill voice, "he released the news on the best goddamn hole I've ever seen. One ounce of gold per ton over eighty feet, if you can believe it!"

When prodded, he explained impatiently that the drill core from the discovery hole at Ptarmigan Mountain had intersected a zone of ore eighty feet thick, containing an average grade of one ounce of gold per ton of rock, an incredible result. "At first I figured it had to be a salt job, but no such luck." He shook his head. "A chance in a goddamn million." He lapsed once more into sullen silence, no doubt imagining what might have been.

"If what you say is true, why do you suppose he did it?"

Pickens shrugged. "To clean up the market before he ran the stock. He knew I had a ton of paper to get off."

"What do you mean?"

Pickens rolled his eyes. "Charlie wanted to concentrate on the exploration side of things, so he contracted me to do the promotion. He optioned me a block of stock as payment. He knew I was hard up at the time, so I guess he was afraid that I'd unload my shares and take my profits as soon as the news was out. He didn't want anybody selling while he was trying to move the stock up."

"Would you have done that?"

"Not on your life! With results that good, I'd have gone along for the ride. The bastard."

"In any case," Powell said, "your rather public feud with Murray was reported in the Vancouver press at the time. And when Murray refused to help you with your latest scheme, in spite of the fact that you had been instrumental in his own success—" Powell paused strategically "—you killed him."

At this, Detective-Sergeant Black looked up from his scribbling, a shaggy eyebrow cocked.

Pickens did not speak for several moments. When he began, his words were surprisingly measured. "Look, Powell, before this thing gets out of hand, I'd better explain a few things. Charlie Murray and I were old friends. Sure, we'd had our differences—it's all part of the game. You win some, you lose some, but you've got to be a big boy about it. You don't go around killing people every time things don't work out. It's true that I went to see Charlie to ask for help. But it wasn't charity I was after— I was prepared to give him a piece of the action. It's also true that he wasn't interested, but he did offer to put me in touch with one of his contacts in London. That's all there was to it. I swear it's the truth." He sagged in his chair, hunched and motionless.

"You say that Murray did not choose to take you up on your offer. Why was that, do you suppose?"

"I don't know. He said he was finished with business. But there was something else. He seemed a little down, you know, depressed. He even talked about selling out and moving back to Vancouver."

This caught Powell's attention. "Really? Did he say why?"

"Not in so many words. But I think he was home-sick, and I got the impression he was worried about his daughter."

"What do you mean?" Powell asked sharply.

"I don't know exactly. I just got the feeling they weren't really happy living in the castle, didn't feel at home, if you know what I mean."

"I see. This contact in London that Murray put you on to, I'd like his name."

Pickens hesitated. "Is it necessary?"

Powell sighed. "Surely you can see that it would be in your best interests if we were able to establish that Charles Murray assisted you by arranging this meeting."

Pickens attempted a smile, although it looked more like a snarl. "You mean it would undermine my supposed motive for killing him."

Powell did not think a reply was necessary.

Pickens leaned forward in his chair with a comically earnest expression. "Let's be reasonable. This guy is a prominent London broker and I'm depending on European financing for Lucky Diamond. Even a hint of scandal would . . . Look, if I give you his name, will you give me your word that you'll tell him no more than is absolutely necessary?"

"You're hardly in a position to be setting down conditions," Powell snapped. "Now, who is it?"

Pickens mumbled a reply.

"Did you get that, Sergeant?"

Black grunted.

"You are free to go, Mr. Pickens. But we'd like to know where you'll be staying for the next few days in case we need to get in touch. Is that a problem?"

Pickens seemed about to protest, but evidently thought better of it. He shook his head.

"Good." Powell stood up abruptly and walked to the door. He stopped and turned at the last moment. "Just one more thing: Did Murray say anything to you about going to meet someone else after he put you on the train?"

Pickens shrugged. "I don't remember. But we'd had a few drinks by then."

"Really? I was given to understand that Murray didn't touch the stuff."

Pickens snorted. "You've got to be kidding. Charlie could carouse with the best of them, although, come to mention it, he did say that he'd been on the wagon since he got over here. But it would have been bad manners to let me get loaded alone, wouldn't it? So we had a little celebration, for old times' sake."

Powell stared at him without speaking.

Pickens squirmed uncomfortably. "I mean, if a man can't have a drink now and then, what's the point?"

What's the bloody point, indeed, Powell thought. "That will be all for now, Mr. Pickens. Sergeant Black will see to you."

Back in his office, Powell placed a call to Dr. Campbell in Grantown. He took pains to put his question as succinctly as possible but was subjected nonetheless to a lengthy dissertation on the intricacies of estimating the relative cooling rates of bodies in air and water in cases where unconsciousness occurs prior to death. In the end he was able to extract an opinion and, after ringing off, sat Buddha-like at his desk for a considerable length of time. He thought about calling Alex, but decided that it could wait. At four o'clock he left for his pub.

* * *

The next morning Powell was in the City amongst the "slovenly towers of commerce," as they had thus been characterized by HRH in those heady days when the poor bloke had little else to worry about save the state of British architecture. Slightly hungover, he was seeking the offices of Pickens's business contact.

When he had arrived home the previous evening, having had considerably more than was sufficient, he had encountered a predictably frosty reception from Marion, who had only just returned home from Ely with the boys. He had risen early while the rest of the household still slept, packing his things as quietly as he could. Before leaving for the office, he had scribbled a guilty note promising to call from the station.

Past the New Stock Exchange, a jog across Throgmorton Street, and Powell eventually located the gleaming steel and glass office tower that housed the offices of Ritchie, Wilson and Moon Investment Securities Limited. He took the lift to the fourteenth floor and was shown into the capacious offices of Mr. Paul Ritchie, senior partner. They shook hands.

"Chief Superintendent, this is indeed a pleasure."

"Thank you for agreeing to see me on such short notice." He was offered a polished leather chair that enveloped him like a womb. Powell took in his surroundings, an Inuit carving here, a Regency table there. Not the sort of operation one would expect to be flogging worthless shares to an unsuspecting public.

"Now, Chief Superintendent, what can we do for Scotland Yard?"

"As I indicated on the telephone . . ."

Ritchie had turned his attention to the computer terminal on his desk. His fingertips moved deftly over the keyboard. He looked up and smiled. "Commodity quotations. Please forgive me. In this business one gets into the habit of keeping track of several things at once."

"I'll try to be brief, Mr. Ritchie. I understand that you were acquainted with the late Charles Murray."

Ritchie frowned, absently rubbing a graying temple. "Yes, a terrible tragedy, simply terrible. I just spoke to him a week ago. I still can't believe it."

"What precisely was the nature of your relationship?"

"Relationship?" Ritchie looked slightly puzzled. "We were business associates. Over the years my firm has been involved in arranging European financing for a number of Charles's projects, mostly through private share placements."

"You mean that you raised money for Murray by recruiting individuals to purchase shares in his various companies?"

"That's basically it, yes."

"I'll get right to the point, Mr. Ritchie. I am told that penny mining shares of the type promoted by Charles Murray are rather risky investments. Would you agree?"

Ritchie smiled affably. "Very delicately put, Chief Superintendent, but quite correct. The other side of the coin, of course, is that the returns can be spectacular. But you have to know what you're doing."

"Oh, yes?"

"I can speak only for my firm, of course, but, first and foremost, we avoid paper promotions; we look for projects that have real merit. And before we invest in any junior mining company we carefully consider the various factors involved: the geological setting of the property, the track record and integrity of the promoters, various technical indicators, the risk tolerance of the client, and so forth. However, to put the matter into perspective, speculative securities of this type would normally account for less than five percent of our clients' portfolios."

Powell was skeptical. "What about the penny share scandals one is always hearing about?"

"There are far too many scams, I would agree. But it's difficult to quantify the problem because the market in penny shares tends to be highly volatile at the best of times."

Powell's expression evinced obvious puzzlement.

Ritchie smiled patiently. "It all boils down to liquidity, or, simply put, the ease with which one can buy or sell a commodity in the marketplace. In the equity markets this is basically a function of the supply of shares. Take a highly capitalized blue chip company, for instance. There will be hundreds of millions of shares outstanding; millions of shares may change hands each day. Generally speaking, the activities of a few traders cannot materially affect either the supply or demand, or consequently the price of the shares. It takes many buyers and sellers—a majority opinion, if you like—to effect a trend one way or the other.

"Junior issues are another matter entirely. The typical penny stock will have less than ten million free-trading shares, and it's not unusual for a stock listed on a junior exchange, say Vancouver or Alberta, to trade only a few thousand shares a day, if at all. Because the supply of shares is so limited, a relatively small change in the balance of supply and demand can have a dramatic effect on the share price. So you can appreciate that it would be very difficult to prove whether a particular price move was due to market manipulation by insiders, or just normal volatility." He paused and placed his fingertips together. "The bottom line, Mr. Powell, if you will forgive a banality, is caveat emptor."

"Mr. Ritchie, you said that your firm looks for legitimate projects to invest in, yet you've also hinted at the importance of promotion. It's the promoter's role I'm wondering about. It seems to me that a legitimate company should be able to attract investors without having to hire someone to tout its shares. Am I missing something?"

"In a word, yes. In the mining business you have to spend a lot of money on exploration and development before you know whether or not you have a mine. The promoter's job is to create an audience for the company's story. Promotion is a dirty word in some circles, but it is nothing more than a vehicle for raising capital. Without capital, work cannot be done, and if work cannot be done, there is no way to turn a project's potential into reality. There are literally hundreds of small exploration companies out there competing for the investor's attention. No one is going to beat a path to your door—you have to knock on theirs."

"Why then do promoters have such an unsavory reputation?"

"It's a wild and wooly world out there, Mr. Powell. The mineral exploration business is one of the last refuges of unfettered capitalism and, given the stakes involved, one can see the potential for exaggeration, outright lies, and even fraud. Having said that, however, the majority of promoters in my experience play by the rules."

"What about Charles Murray?"

"He was one of the best."

But at what? wondered Powell. "You mentioned that you spoke to Murray recently. What was the subject of your conversation?"

"Charles called to introduce an acquaintance of his who is in the UK trying to raise some capital for a Canadian diamond project. Naturally, as a favor to Charles, I agreed to see this chap. He's coming in to see me this afternoon, as a matter of fact." Ritchie shrugged. "Apart from the usual chitchat, that was about it."

Powell had to restrain himself from delving into the subject of Oliver Pickens, but he decided that Ritchie was capable of looking after himself. Besides, it was time to come to the point. "Tell me, Mr. Ritchie, in your professional capacity as a stock broker, can you think of any way that somebody might have profited from Charles Murray's death?"

"You mean apart from his heirs and successors?" He appeared to consider the matter carefully. "I suppose anyone who was short the shares of any of the companies in which Charles had an interest."

Once again Powell raised a quizzical eyebrow.

Ritchie smiled. "Short selling is an investment strategy whereby one can capitalize on a decline in the price of a company's shares. The short seller borrows the shares, in effect, and then sells them in the expectation that the price will fall. He hopes to buy the shares back at a lower price—or cover his position, as we say in the trade—to return them to their owner and pocket the difference as his profit. Of course, if the price of the shares goes up, the shorts lose money. In the case of a junior company, if a high-profile promoter were to, er, suddenly disappear from the scene, it is likely that the share price would plummet, at least in the short term, resulting in large profits for anyone who was short the stock."

"But would that really apply in Charles Murray's case? I understood that he was retired."

Ritchie smiled expansively. "Men like Charles Murray never really retire, Mr. Powell. Charles still had a few irons in the fire. But more to the point, he was still a major shareholder in a number of exploration companies, which lent an element of credibility to their various projects. Let me illustrate my point." Ritchie punched something into his computer. "Ah, here it is. Aurora Mining Corporation, Charles's flagship company, is down another quarter this morning. Since the announcement of Charles's death last week, the shares are off nearly thirty percent. Some of the other stocks are down even more."

"Would it be possible to determine who was selling a particular stock short?"

"It should be possible, since just about everything nowadays is stored in a computer somewhere. But you'd have to contact the Canadian securities authorities for that kind of information."

"For a start, would you be able to provide me with a list of the companies with which Murray was associated?"

"I'll see what I can do. Would tomorrow afternoon be soon enough, say three o'clock?"

"Fine. I'll have my assistant, Sergeant Black, drop by." Powell hesitated for a moment. "I don't mind telling you that considerable pressure is being exerted on us through diplomatic channels to clear this matter up as quickly as possible. Does that surprise you?"

Ritchie regarded Powell carefully before replying. "Despite his humble beginnings, Charles Murray was a member of the Canadian establishment. You might even say that he had friends in high places. Some of these people would undoubtedly have had a financial interest in Charles's various ventures. As a result of his death, considerable sums of money have been lost, at least on paper. So the sooner this matter is—if you'll forgive me—laid to rest, the happier everyone will be. Even more than bad news, Mr. Powell, investors abhor uncertainty."

"The same can be said of policemen," Powell replied dryly. He rose to leave. "I won't keep you any longer, Mr. Ritchie. You've been most helpful."

"Not at all. You know, Mr. Powell, it occurs to me that your job is not unlike mine."

"How is that?"

"The main problem in both instances is to separate the wheat from the chaff, is it not?"

Powell smiled. "Oh, there is one more thing . . ."

Ritchie looked up from the monitor to which his attention had already returned. "Yes?"

"I think I'll advise my old mum to keep her savings under the mattress."

Ritchie laughed good-naturedly, with just the slightest hint, Powell fancied, of the gleaming canine.

"Very wise, Chief Superintendent, very wise, indeed."

CHAPTER 11

PC Shand was waiting at Aviemore station when the InterCity arrived from London at eight-thirty the next morning. It was obvious that the young constable was fairly bursting with news. While Shand dodged traffic, Powell described in considerably more detail than was absolutely necessary some of the finer points related to the cooling rates of cadavers he had gleaned from Dr. Campbell.

"Any news on the home front?" he inquired when he had made his point.

"Well, sir, I interviewed the downstairs contingent at Castle Glyn and was able to confirm that Murray didn't say anything to anyone about expecting another visitor. But there is one thing that came to light. Apparently Murray kept all of the staff on when he came to Castle Glyn, with one exception. Old Ross's mother, the cook."

"You mean he sacked her?"

"Not exactly. According to Ross, she'd been looking forward to retirement for some time, but hadn't wanted to leave the old laird. She's almost ninety, so I gather it was a mutually agreeable arrangement. Still, I got the impression that Ross resented it."

Powell grunted. "Anything else?" He was certain there was better to come.

"Yes, sir. I also questioned the hotel guests. It seems that the night of the murder was an eventful one at the Salar Lodge."

"What do you mean?" Powell asked, puzzled, as he had been there himself at the time. Then he remembered that he had retired early that first evening.

"According to Mr. Preston—you know, the chap from Zimbabwe—there was a terrible row."

Powell knew Preston only slightly as an atrocious fly caster who nevertheless managed to catch more salmon every year than the other, more polished members of his regular party combined.

"Mr. Preston," Shand continued, "had occasion to be in the front hall of the hotel on his way to the gents at approximately ten-thirty, when a man burst in the front door demanding to see Mr. Whitely, Senior. Mr. Whitely appeared on the scene in due course and escorted this individual into his private office. According to Mr. Preston, there was a loud carfluffle lasting several minutes, after which time the man reappeared and left the premises as abruptly as he had arrived." PC Shand paused a moment, as if for dramatic effect. "The thing is, Mr. Powell, Preston has identified the man as Charles Murray."

Powell showed little reaction. "How does he know it was Murray?"

"He recognized him afterward from the picture in the newspaper."

"Was he able to overhear anything that was said?"

"After making the point that he was not a man to stick his nose in other people's affairs, he did indicate that he heard Murray threaten to put the Salar Lodge out of business, or words to that effect."

As it happened, Powell was not particularly surprised by this revelation. To a degree at least, Nigel's behavior was now explicable. "Well, Shand, the plot thickens. Have you been able to confirm Preston's account?"

"There were a number of other guests in the bar at the time, as well as George Stuart. They all report hearing the disturbance when Murray came into the hotel and again when he left. But none of them actually saw him, nor could anyone confirm Mr. Preston's report of the goings-on in Mr. Whitely's office. I didn't question Mr. Whitely—I assumed that you'd want to do that, sir."

Powell lapsed into reverie. Like objects momentarily illuminated in a car's headlamps, new developments in an investigation were often more enigmatic than revealing. It was clear that Murray could have made life very difficult for Nigel by canceling the agreement granting the Salar Lodge's fishing rights, but the really interesting question was: Why would Murray threaten Nigel in the first place? Powell occupied himself for the remainder of the journey mulling over the various permutations and combinations.

When they arrived at the Salar Lodge, Powell learned from Nigel that Pinky and John Sanders had departed for their beat half an hour earlier. Nigel also indicated, in response to Powell's casual query, that young Bob was off fishing on one of the local hill lochs. After a brief conference with PC Shand, Powell set out in his Triumph with the top down and Van Morrison on the tape deck, but heading not, he suspected, into the mystic.

A blustery wind was whipping up storm caps on Lochindorb as Powell traversed the desolate moors surrounding the loch. With its ruined island castle that had once been inhabited by a charming character known as the Wolf of Badenoch—whose chief pastimes had apparently been raping and pillaging, and who had ultimately suffered the karmic indignity of having a bar in Aviemore named for him—the loch's black depths seemed quite capable of concealing a monster or two. Much like the problem at hand, Powell thought grimly.

Leaving the loch behind, the road climbed steeply beside a little burn that cascaded merrily from pool to pool amongst the heather. Soon the road was reduced to a rough track snaking over the moors. After a few jarring scrapes to the undercarriage of his car, Powell pulled off to the side, having decided that it would be more prudent to continue on foot. Small patches of snow still clung to the steep north face of the pass ahead, across which the track could be seen to switchback dizzily. He consulted his Ordnance Survey map. As he was still some distance from the pass, he decided to take a shortcut over the prominent ridge that bounded on the east the narrow glen up which he had just come. Recalling his Cambridge climbing days, he drew a hearty breath. A bit of scrambling would do him good—get the blood pumping to the essential extremities.

After packing his rucksack with an anorak, a pair of binoculars, some sandwiches, and a small flask for the fortification that was in it, he set off on a long diagonal ascent toward the crest of the ridge. He climbed steadily, breathing hard and sweating profusely. The air was still and stifling. The high corries seemed to reflect and concentrate the intense, unfiltered sunlight, and Powell felt a little like an ant under some malicious boy's magnifying glass. Periodically, the silence was punctuated by a curlew's plaintive cry.

As he climbed, the heather thinned and eventually gave way to a carpet of wiry grass. The crest of the ridge was now only a few yards above him. He paused to catch his breath. Looking back, he could see the track winding across the green smudge of heather beside the silver thread of the burn, but he could no longer pick out the glint of sunlight off his car. Forming a daunting backdrop across the glen, an austere wall of granite breached only by a near-vertical gulley rose for several hundred feet above its base of scree. Without conscious effort he began plotting a route up the face: a layback up that crack, an exposed traverse to the right into the main gulley, and then straight up. The overhang just below the top would be the crux, and the thing was, you wouldn't know until you got there whether you'd be able to do it and by then you'd be more or less committed. Who said climbing wasn't a metaphor for life?

When Powell scrambled onto the broken crest of the ridge a few minutes later, he was greeted by a quenching breeze. He collapsed onto the nearest flattish spot. Before him lay the most fetching prospect. The curve of the valley below was like a great green bowl, rising on the far side to a rocky ridge similar to the one on which he was perched. Hidden behind the ridge lay the valley of the Spey and, beyond that, peak after peak of lighter and lighter blue as far as the eye could see. In the center of the bowl, sunlight gleamed off a small loch. Through the glasses he could make out a white van parked at the water's edge and a small boat plying the surface of the loch. Reluctantly, he got to his feet and began a zigzagging descent, rejoining the track along the shore of the loch.

The occupant of the boat had spotted him and was rowing smartly toward shore. A few minutes later Powell seized the bow line as the boat slid onto the shingled beach.

"Hello, Bob. How's fishing?"

"This is a surprise, Mr. Powell." If young Whitely was in fact surprised to see him, he didn't seem very pleased about it.

In the bottom of the boat lay as pretty a basket of trout as Powell had ever seen. Six fish, each about two pounds, with burnished sides and spots as red as rowanberries.

"You don't know how lucky you are, Bob, living up here like a laird."

"It's all right." He didn't seem altogether convinced of his good fortune.

"Bob, I'd like to have a word."

Whitely clambered out of the boat. "Aye, well, I suppose this is as good a time as any."

Powell sat down in the heather and offered his flask.

Whitely shook his head, sat down himself, and waited.

"Do you come up here often?"

"Not often. Only when I want to get away from people."

Powell nodded, ignoring the barb. "I know what you mean."

"Do you?"

"Look, Bob, I won't bore you with a long speech

about a policeman's duty, because it wouldn't alter the fact that I need to ask you some questions. All right?"

Whitely nodded, revealing no hint of any underlying emotion. Powell had a hunch, however, that this was only a temporary condition. He took a deep breath and plunged in. "How long have you been romantically involved with Heather Murray?"

Whitely flushed and clenched his fists. Instinctively, Powell tensed.

"Who told you?" Whitely whispered hoarsely.

"Let's just say I put two and two together," Powell lied.

"What of it? I've got nothing to hide." There was defiance in his tone.

"I sincerely hope not. After all, her father's just been murdered." Powell suddenly felt weary. "Let's not go all around the houses, Bob. Why don't you tell me about it?" But even as he said the words, he knew that he didn't really want to know.

Whitely stared out over the loch for a few moments. The wind had picked up and little wavelets were slapping rhythmically against the stern of the boat. Eventually he spoke. "When Heather and her old man came over from Canada last summer, they stayed at the hotel for a few days while the renovations were being completed at Castle Glyn. He seemed all right at first, which just goes to show how misleading first impressions can be. But Heather, she was—" he groped for a word "—something else." He shrugged. "One thing led to another and we began seeing each other." His expression suddenly twisted into a mask of pure malice. "Everything was fine 'til he tried to put a stop to it."

"I assume you're referring to Mr. Murray?"

Whitely spat, "Who else?"

"I don't understand, Bob. You're both adults—what could he do?"

"You didn't know him, Mr. Powell. He didn't get where he did in life by letting other people have their way."

"How did Heather—Miss Murray—react?"

Whitely shook his head disgustedly. "I don't know. I think she felt some sort of misguided loyalty, a duty to look after him in his dotage or some such rubbish. Because of her mum and all that."

"A perfectly natural way for a daughter to feel about her father, don't you think?"

Whitely scowled but said nothing.

"Did you and Miss Murray continue to see each other?"

"No, we—I mean, Heather thought it best not to for a while."

"Tell me, did anything happen recently, say in the last month or so, to alter the picture?"

"I don't know what you mean."

"I understand that Murray had been considering returning to Canada."

"What gave you that idea?" Whitely said sharply.

"Is it true?"

"I think Heather might have mentioned it," he admitted grudgingly. "What difference does it make?"

"Do you think Miss Murray would have gone with her father?"

"You'd have to ask her about that."

"I'll do that. Look, Bob, I'm afraid it's my duty to inquire as to your whereabouts last week Monday."

"What?" Whitely seemed slightly irritated by the question. "You know I didn't get back from Aberdeen until the next day."

"Yes, of course. Did you know that Murray paid a visit to the Salar Lodge on that Monday night, shortly before he was killed?"

"How could I?"

"What would you say if I told you that Murray was overheard making certain threats to your father?"

"I'd say I didn't know a thing about it, but I wouldn't put it past him."

"What do you mean?"

"Look, I've already told you he was a rotten bastard."

Powell sighed. He'd always been fond of the lad, but his patience was beginning to wear a bit thin. "Is there anything else you'd like to tell me, Bob? Anything at all?"

Whitely shook his head sullenly.

Powell glanced significantly at his watch. "Well, I'd better be getting back, then. I've a long tramp ahead of me." He straightened slowly with, he hoped, a discernible creaking of joints.

There was an awkward interval in which neither man spoke.

"Here, I'll give you a lift," Whitely mumbled.

After packing up, they drove in strained silence back to Powell's car. Along Lochindorb, Whitely's white van overtook Powell's Triumph and sped away, spraying the little roadster with gravel.

In Kinlochy, Powell stopped at Grant and Son's Tackle Shop to purchase some flies in the faint but rapidly dwindling hope that he might someday soon have an opportunity to use them. As he entered the shop he nearly collided with John Sanders, who was just leaving with a long rod tube in hand. Sanders looked startled.

"Erskine, fancy bumping into you like this! I haven't had a chance to thank you. The fishing's been so good that I've decided to stay on for a few more days. That is, I mean if it's all right . . ."

"Of course," Powell said. "The way things are going, I expect I'll be tied up for a while yet."

"Pinky's told me all about the case. Busman's holiday, eh? Any suspects yet? No? Well, tell you what, I'll pop over to the hotel one evening and buy you a drink. Thank you properly."

"I'll take you up on that."

"It's settled then. See you."

"Right."

Old Peter Grant, something of a local institution, was muttering to himself behind the cluttered counter. "Ber-luddy daft, more money than brains, ber-luddy Yanks."

"What seems to be the trouble, Mr. Grant?"

"Ye saw that gent that just walked oot?"

"Mr. Sanders? Yes, I know him."

"It's nae business of mine what company ye keep."

Powell had to make an effort to keep a straight face. "What did he do exactly, Mr. Grant?"

"Weel, he comes in here aboot a week ago tae buy a new salmon rod. Says he's never used one before. So I fixed him up wi' a fifteen-foot carbon fiber. One of my own custom jobs and a real beauty it was, too. Then what does he do? He comes in today and says he's broken it. Wants tae buy a new one, he says." He glared at Powell triumphantly.

"So?"

Grant shook his grizzled head, as if wondering how anybody could be so thick. "The rod blank is guaranteed by the makers, so I told him tae bring back the pieces and I'd gladly replace the rod. Free of charge," he added significantly, as if that explained everything. "Ye'll not believe what he said. He said it was his own fault and he'd thrown the pieces away. Said he wanted tae buy a new one."

Powell was no longer listening as Grant blethered on about the dire consequences of rampant profligacy to civilization as we know it. Instead, he walked out of the shop, having forgotten about the dozen Munro Killers in assorted sizes and thereby reinforcing the old man's opinion of all foreigners.

CHAPTER 12

It was going on four o'clock when Powell got back to the hotel. One look at Ruby's face and he knew that something was terribly amiss.

"Oh, Mr. Powell, I don't know what to say!"

Powell steeled himself reflexively. "What is it, Ruby? What's wrong?"

"It's Mr. Warburton! Mr. Preston and young Mr. Crawford pulled him from the river an hour ago—"

Powell felt a cold hand clutch his heart. "Is he—"

"He's alive, thank the good Lord." She produced a voluminous handkerchief and blew her nose noisily. "They brought him back to the hotel, all of them soaked to the skin and Mr. Warburton gasping and sputtering something awful. Half drowned he was, Mr. Powell, and terrible blue in the face. I called Dr. Webster right away."

Powell felt a surge of relief. "Where is he now?"

"They took him to hospital in Grantown."

Powell nodded. Suddenly, something occurred to him. "Where's Mr. Sanders?"

She seemed puzzled. "Now that you mention it, I haven't seen him all afternoon."

Powell noticed for the first time how terrible Ruby looked. Her eyes were red rimmed and swollen and her plump face was almost white. He placed his hand lightly on her shoulder.

"This must be very upsetting for you, Ruby. Do you have any idea what happened?"

She looked at Powell uncomprehendingly for a moment. Then she spoke in a barely audible whisper, "First Mr. Murray and now Mr. Warburton."

Powell removed his hand. Feeling curiously detached, he heard himself speak. "Ruby, what are you saying?"

She clutched his hand in both of hers and looked up at him like a wounded deer. "Oh, Mr. Powell! What does it all mean?"

Powell stared at her, not knowing what to think. "I don't know; I honestly don't know." He gently pried his fingers from her grasp. "I must get to the hospital. Does Nigel know?"

Ruby seemed unable to speak, her mouth opening and closing soundlessly. "He—he went out after lunch and hasn't come back." Her voice broke. It was obvious that she was terrified.

After inquiring at Admittance, Powell ran up the stairs to the second floor. An elderly, tweedy-looking man had just emerged from the last room on the right at the end of the corridor.

"Dr. Webster?"

"Aye?"

Powell produced his identification. "I've come to see about Mr. Warburton . . ." He left it open ended.

Webster squinted myopically at Powell's card and then frowned. "You're a long way from home, Chief Superintendent. May I ask if your interest in Mr. Warburton's condition is a professional one?"

"He's a friend."

"I see. Well, he's had a nasty experience. He's a very lucky man, in fact." As if sensing the contradiction, he added irritably, "Another few minutes in that cold water and, well, who knows?"

"How is he?"

"He'll survive."

Charming bedside manner. "How long will he have to stay here?"

"A day or two, just to make certain that there are no complications."

"May I see him?"

Dr. Webster regarded Powell severely, like a schoolmaster sizing up an errant boy. He glanced at his watch. "Fifteen minutes and not a minute more." With that he strode ramrod-straight down the corridor, leaving Powell alone with the echoing footsteps and hospital smells.

Warburton lay still with his eyes closed, his round face uncharacteristically pale against the dingy pillowcase. His breathing was labored and uneven. As Powell closed the door quietly behind him, Warburton began to cough violently, gasping raspingly between paroxysms as if unable to catch his breath. Powell bounded to his bedside and helped him sit up.

"Easy does it, old chap."

Powell propped him up with the pillow and then

poured a glass of water from a stainless steel pitcher on the bedside table. When the fit had subsided, Warburton drank greedily. Eventually, he managed a weak smile.

"Thanks, I needed that, although God knows I've swallowed enough water for a lifetime."

"I came as quickly as I could. You can't imagine how I feel, Pinky, if only I'd been . . ."

"Nonsense. I'll pull through. Could have happened to anybody. Simply a matter of being in the wrong place at the right time. The main thing is to find out who did it, so that it doesn't happen to anyone else."

The import of Warburton's words caught Powell like a blow to the solar plexus. Until that moment he had refused to acknowledge that Pinky's mishap could have been anything but an accident. Confronted earlier with Ruby's fears, he had preferred to think that she had simply been caught up in the emotion of the moment and had let her imagination get the better of her. But once again it seemed that Ruby's intuition was uncannily sound. He felt a wave of anger rising like bile at the back of his throat. It was personal now, and he promised himself that he'd leave no stone unturned. Grim faced, he drew up a chair and asked quietly, "How did it happen?"

"Where to begin?" Warburton shook his head sheepishly. "You know, it's funny. One always supposes, rather immodestly I daresay, that if one were ever placed in a situation like this, one would give one's statement clearly and succinctly and without emotion. But to be honest, Erskine, my mind is in complete turmoil."

Powell said reassuringly, "First off, Pinky, you are not being cross-examined. Secondly, you've just been through a terrible ordeal, so take your time and do the best you can."

Warburton smiled wanly. "Thanks, old chap." He closed his eyes momentarily, as if to distill his thoughts. "We'd drawn the bridge beat," he began slowly. "The water was fishing well and we'd each had a fish in the morning. When we returned to the beat after lunch, poached plaice and a rather respectable hock—" he digressed a trifle wistfully "—I elected to fish the Bridge Pool, and John decided to try his luck down by the birch spinney. After an hour or so, I stopped for some refreshment. John joined me presently and said he had to pop into town to run some errands."

"Before you continue, Pinky, tell me how you got to your beat today."

"We've been taking turns driving. It was John's turn today, so we took his car in the morning. But after lunch he suggested that we each take our own vehicle, which suited me fine." He grimaced. "John has hired one of those cramped little tin cans like Alex's and one feels a bit like a sardine. At any rate, where was I? Oh, yes— after John had gone I fished through the pool once more and then decided to move a little farther downstream. I was bringing in my line when I hooked on to something. At first I thought I'd snagged bottom, but when I pulled hard the thing came loose and eventually I managed to get it in."

Warburton lapsed into another coughing fit. Waving Powell off, he took several deep, ragged breaths and then clutched Powell's sleeve. "It was the rod!" he whispered hoarsely.

"What?"

"The one left behind by Arthur's poacher. It must have

been. It was a double-hander with the reel and line still attached. There was no sign of corrosion, so it couldn't have been in the water very long."

"That was a bit of luck," Powell said distractedly. The police divers had combed the river for two days and hadn't come up with a thing. Still, it was the same with drownings—the bodies often turned up when you least expected them. An article like a fishing rod could, he supposed, get lodged in various places in a large river where it would be difficult to spot. First Murray's corpse and now this. It seemed that the salmon rod would soon replace the grapple for dredging up clues from the deeps. "Did you happen to notice the make?" he asked.

Pinky smiled. "You know I always notice that sort of thing. As a matter of fact, it was a very nice custom job by that local maker, Peter Grant."

Powell felt his jaw tighten. That drink with John Sanders had suddenly shot to the top of his social agenda. "Are you certain?"

Warburton looked mildly surprised. "Of course. His name was on it, signed in India ink just above the grip."

Powell nodded. "Go on."

"I was sitting on that big rock at the bottom end of the pool examining the rod when, without any hint of a warning, someone pushed me from behind. The next thing I knew, I was in the drink and it was bloody cold, I can tell you." He shivered convulsively.

"Did you get a look at him?"

"Afraid not, old man. I was too busy swimming for dear life. The current was faster than it looked and there was a strong undertow. All I can remember is a loud roaring sound in my ears. The next thing I knew, I was being revived by Preston and young Crawford."

"What happened to the rod?"

Warburton shrugged. "It's at the bottom of the river again, I expect."

"Do you have any idea what time all this happened?"

"I'd only be guessing, but I'd say near enough three."

"How long after Sanders had left for town would that be?"

"Ten or fifteen minutes, I should think." Warburton tossed Powell a curious glance. "Why do you ask?"

"Force of habit. By the way, have you heard from Sanders?"

Warburton shook his head. "I'm a bit puzzled about that, actually. When he got back he must have wondered what had happened to me. I've been expecting him to pop in."

"Bloody peculiar, I'd say. You wouldn't happen to know what he does by way of earning a crust, would you?"

"I haven't the faintest idea. He seldom talks about himself, and one doesn't like to pry."

"Pinky, did you happen to mention Arthur's run-in with the poacher to Sanders?"

Pinky looked guilty. "Shouldn't I have?"

"It's not important." Powell tried to think. Something was nagging away at the back of his brain, but for the life of him he couldn't put his finger on it.

On his way back to the Salar Lodge, Powell paid a visit to the Ravenscroft Guesthouse. The proprietor, a Mrs. Blakey, informed him that, yes, Mr. Sanders was staying there, but, no, he was not in at the moment. And, no, sir, not a word to the gentleman. Powell had created the impression that he was an old friend who wanted to surprise Sanders.

Barrett rang as usual that evening and after Powell had brought him up to date, the Scot described in minute detail what he would do if he ever got his hands on Pinky's assailant.

"The main thing is he's all right," Barrett concluded, "but this certainly puts matters in a different light. I can finish up here tomorrow and—" He hesitated. "Look, Erskine, why don't I call in someone from Division to help out?" He left the rest unsaid.

"Thanks all the same, Alex, but I can manage." Powell's tone left no room for argument.

Barrett was about to say something about the hazards of getting personally involved in a case but decided that it wasn't necessary. He had to assume that Powell knew what he was doing. "Right, then," he said. "Why don't you review what we have so far?"

Powell summarized the facts of the case, scrupulously avoiding any hint of subjectivity.

"Cagey, aren't we?" Barrett observed. "I take it you'd like to hear my views before committing yourself. Well, for what it's worth, my money's still on Pickens. The man seems unwilling or, more likely, unable to provide a proper alibi, and he's admitted that Murray diddled him when they were in business together. So there's both opportunity and motive. And let's not forget that he was, as far as we know, the last person to see Murray alive. But proving it is another thing."

Powell shook his head doubtfully. "I don't know. There's

something about Pickens that rings true. When I was inter-viewing him I got the distinct impression that he was more interested in his latest business deal than the possibility of a murder charge."

Barrett was adamant. "That's not inconsistent with the type of character we're dealing with. No, as far as I'm concerned, he's still our best bet."

Powell sighed heavily. "Point made."

"Moving down the list," Barrett said carefully, "we are bound to consider Nigel." He paused to give Powell the opportunity to protest, but when there was no reaction he forged ahead. "Murray threatened to put Nigel out of business mere hours before he was murdered, by reneg-ing on the Salar Lodge's fishing rights. There's a lot of Maggie Whitely in the Salar Lodge, and I'm convinced that Nigel would do anything in his power to protect what they'd built together."

"Including murder?" Powell asked incredulously.

"I know the idea seems ridiculous, but, as you yourself have pointed out, Nigel's been behaving very strangely of late. He'd been through hell with Maggie and now there's the prospect of Bob leaving; perhaps he'd reached the end of his tether. There's another possibility, of course. Nigel may have a good idea who did kill Murray and is profoundly disturbed by the prospect."

"You mean Bob, I take it."

"Murray stood between the lad and his true love, a rather precarious position, I'd say, considering Bob's pen-chant for going off half-cocked. And putting it bluntly, one must also consider the fact that Heather Murray's, em, dowry has increased substantially as a result of her father's death—rather sweetening the pot, in a manner of speak-

ing." He paused significantly and the silence stretched out
awkwardly. Once again, he decided it best to soldier on.
"While we're on the subject, it seems to me that Miss
Murray, herself, is no small enigma. Her devotion to her
father seems rather odd when you consider that he could
apparently be such a bastard. She's admitted they'd had a
major row, quite possibly over her choice of boyfriends,
and she strikes me as the type who's used to having her
own way."

"What are you implying?"

"I am simply drawing your attention to the rich tapes-
try of possibilities that confronts us. Did you know that
ninety percent of all violence in Britain involves family
members?"

Barrett could be a royal pain in the arse at times.

"And finally," he continued with exasperating precision, "there's John Sanders. Now I'll admit that this fishing rod business is suggestive, but it just doesn't stand up
to scrutiny. If Sanders had committed a murder, why in
heaven's name would he stick around? The natural reaction would be to put as many miles between himself and
Kinlochy as quickly as possible. Being a tourist, he could
have slipped away without drawing the slightest attention
to himself.

"Let's assume for the sake of argument that Sanders did
kill Murray and then decided for some inexplicable reason
to linger at the scene of the crime. And let us accept, moreover, that it was in fact Sanders whom Arthur encountered
a few days later, poaching, cool as a cucumber, on his victim's water. The fact remains that the rod found by Pinky,
even supposing it did belong to Sanders, in no way links
him to the murder. A possible conviction on a minor

poaching offense hardly seems a sufficient motive for attempting to kill Pinky."

"That doesn't alter the fact that somebody tried to."

"Well, what do *you* suggest?"

"The one thing consistently lacking in this case is hard evidence. So, first off, we need to get the boffins combing the ground around the Old Bridge."

"Right."

"And I'm going to have a little chat with Sanders. I'm still convinced that there's more to our Canadian friend than meets the eye. In the meantime, why don't you punch him into your computer and see what you come up with."

"Anything else, *mein Kapitän*?"

"That should do it. Oh, yes, we'd better have another go at Pickens. I'll have Sergeant Black pull him in again and wring him dry. Now, if there's nothing else, I'm going to repair to the bar for a nightcap."

"First things first. You didn't think that I was going to let you off the hook that easily, did you?" Barrett prodded.

"I beg your pardon?"

"I stuck my neck out. Now it's your turn."

Powell sighed. "Well, I won't quibble with anything you've said, but there is one person you haven't mentioned."

"And who might that be?"

"Ruby."

"You're joking, surely."

"I'm convinced that she's trying to shield one or both of the Whitelys. Think about it. Her first reaction after learning of Charles Murray's disappearance was to report it to a policeman. Then she seemed to go out of her way to imply, without actually saying so, that Murray was something of a lush, someone who might be expected to get into a bit of trouble now and then. Yet according to his daughter, he was on the wagon."

"It's obvious that somebody's not telling the truth."

"On the contrary, I think both statements are entirely consistent."

"What exactly are you driving at?"

"Simply this: When Ruby first heard about Murray's disappearance, I think she suspected the worst. Furthermore, I think she had some reason to speculate about the identity of his killer. To ease her conscience, perhaps, she made a token effort to bring the matter to our attention, but once she'd done her duty she did her best to suggest an alternative explanation for Murray's disappearance. I believe Ruby knew through her friendship with Heather Murray that Charles Murray had once been a hard drinker; I think she wanted desperately to believe Murray had reverted to his old ways and had met his end as a result of some sort of accident."

"But aren't you forgetting that Murray *had* been drinking on the night he was killed?" Barrett protested.

"Pure coincidence. Look, we know he was considering chucking it all and returning to Canada. He'd just had a row with his daughter when his old mate Oliver Pickens drops in to reminisce about the good old days. It's hardly surprising he fell off the wagon."

Barrett grunted irritably. "This is getting us nowhere fast."

"You asked."

After disconnecting, Powell rang up the Ravenscroft

Guesthouse and learned from Mrs. Blakey that Sanders had still not returned. Next he called Shand and arranged to have the guesthouse placed under surveillance, leaving strict orders to be notified the moment Sanders put in an appearance. Best not to set the cat amongst the pigeons just yet.

Having fulfilled his professional obligations, he made a beeline for the bar, where he spent the remainder of the evening debating the merits of the dry fly for Scottish salmon with George, the bartender. At ten forty-five he received word that Sanders had returned to the guesthouse. A quick call to Mrs. Blakey revealed that Sanders had already retired. "Without even taking his tea," she added significantly.

"I'll surprise him tomorrow morning, then, Mrs. Blakey."

"Och, you are a one, Mr. Powell," she chortled.

"Not half, Mrs. Blakey, not bloody half," he muttered after he'd rung off.

CHAPTER 13

When Powell arrived at the Old Bridge the next morning, the scene-of-crime lads were already hard at it. As he walked down to the river he made a mental note to have Pinky's Land Rover driven back to the hotel. PC Shand introduced Powell to Inspector McInnes, who was in charge of operations. McInnes was a wiry man with restless blue eyes that didn't miss a thing. He exuded an air of quiet competence and Powell liked him immediately.

"Anything, yet?" Powell asked.

"We've found a fishing rod, sir," McInnes replied smartly. "Lying on the shingle, over there by the big rock."

"Let's have a look at it."

A salmon rod was produced, and one glance told Powell what he wanted to know. "That's Mr. Warburton's rod. We're looking for a custom job, similar in length and general appearance, but made by Peter Grant of Kinlochy. It probably went into the river with Mr. Warburton."

"I'll get a couple of my men to suit up right away."

"Anything else?"

McInnes shrugged. "The usual paraphernalia, bits of discarded line, the odd broken hook, cigarette butts, plastic wrappers, broken glass, and the like. Nothing out of the ordinary."

After a brief consultation with McInnes, Powell and Shand donned chest-high waders at the river's edge. Powell pointed to a large, flat-topped rock that lay half submerged approximately twenty feet from where they stood, where the river narrowed slightly after debouching from the Bridge Pool.

"Right, once I get settled out there, I want you to wade out as quietly as you can, just like you were sneaking up on me, then give me a tap on the back."

"Yes, sir," Shand said doubtfully.

Powell began to slosh his way through the shallows. He was soon up to his crotch and could feel the river sucking the warmth from his legs through the waders's thin rubber membrane. The current was stronger than it looked, and he had to move carefully over the algae-smeared cobbles. When he reached the rock, he clambered up without too much difficulty and settled himself on his slick perch with his back to the others, legs dangling in the current. The river bottom dropped off steeply before him into the main flow of the river. He called out to PC Shand, "Right."

He closed his eyes, relaxed yet fully alert, and immersed himself in the sounds around him. He could distinguish the lapping of wavelets against the rock, the powerful suck of the current as it funneled past him, and the muted roar of distant rapids, harmoniously married like the notes of a liquid chord. Occasionally he caught a snatch of conversation from McInnes's men.

Powell was jarred from his meditation by a loud splash. Startled, he resisted the temptation to open his eyes. A salmon must have jumped in the Bridge Pool. He steadied himself again.

The next thing he knew, he was in the water, thrashing wildly and fighting to stay on his feet as the current swept him downstream. The water lapped at the top of his waders and he could feel the sobering shock of the first icy trickles running down his legs. He tried to steer toward the bank by keeping his feet moving on the shifting cobbles as if he were running down a scree, but as he took on more and more water, his waders began to pull him down like a deadweight. He was struggling desperately now but was unable to make any shoreward progress. With a curious sense of detachment he realized that he was being forced inexorably into deeper and faster water. Powell was vaguely aware of men shouting and felt faintly ridiculous as he contemplated the possible ignominious consequences of his little lark. In keeping with the gravity of the situation he fancied he could hear the faint skirling of bagpipes. He thought about Marion and the boys and felt the sharp edge of panic at his throat.

He was about to cry out when something caught his arm from behind and he found himself staring into the taut face of Inspector McInnes. Clutching each other and lurching like two drunks, Powell and McInnes managed with their combined strength to stem the current and edge crablike toward shore. When they reached the shallows, they collapsed together and crawled on their hands and knees onto the shingle, fully spent, like a pair of beached whales. In a clumsy slow-motion ballet Powell struggled out of his waders and rolled onto his back, gasping for breath.

McInnes, ashen faced, inquired anxiously, "Are you all right, Mr. Powell? My God, you might have drowned!" His expression suddenly darkened. "Bloody hell!"

"Forget it—no harm done," Powell said heartily, or as near to it as he could manage under the circumstances. He pushed himself into a sitting position. "By the way, thanks." He winced as he slowly flexed his cramping legs.

There was a great commotion as McInnes's men, with Shand in tow, descended upon them. A large plaid blanket and an unofficial medicinal flask were produced, and Powell and McInnes huddled for a few moments in the warm afterglow of these ministrations. Then McInnes fixed PC Shand with a withering stare. "You had better explain yourself, Constable."

Shand, who looked more miserable and bedraggled than either of the casualties, said haltingly, "I didn't mean— I mean, I didn't realize it was so slippery. I lost my footing as I reached out to touch Mr. Powell. The next thing I knew . . ." Shand looked at Powell with a pathetic expression, visions of his erstwhile career evaporating before his eyes. "I—I'm terribly sorry, sir."

Before Powell could respond, McInnes asked incredulously, "But why did you just stand there gawking, man?"

PC Shand's expression evinced utter and total devastation. "I—I'm afraid of the water, sir," he stammered.

"What?" McInnes roared.

Shand repeated himself, more piteously than before.

"Well, laddie," McInnes rumbled ominously, "we'll

soon rectify that particular deficiency in your training. I'll see to it personally."

It was learned in the discussion that followed that something of interest had turned up on the road. One of McInnes's men, a Sergeant Cavers, stepped forward to elaborate.

"Based on my examination, sir, I have identified three distinct sets of tire impressions in the turnaround area, possibly four. All are fairly fresh, made in the last day or so, I'd say. One set, of course, belongs to the Land Rover that's parked up there, another set appears to have been made by a subcompact model, and the third by a vehicle with a longer wheel base. A small lorry or possibly a van would be my guess."

Powell and Shand exchanged involuntary glances.

"Is it possible to determine the sequence of comings and goings?" Powell asked.

Cavers frowned. "It's difficult, sir. The ground is badly churned up with the recent rain, but it does appear that the impressions made by the smaller vehicle were superimposed on the other two."

"You mentioned the possibility of a fourth set of tracks."

"Yes, sir. There is another, very faint impression on the harder, drier ground just before you get to the turnaround, but it's difficult to say how old it is. Another small car, it looks like."

Powell nodded. "Good work, Sergeant. You've taken some photographs, I presume?"

"Yes, sir."

Powell emerged somewhat reluctantly from his tartan cocoon and got to his feet with an undignified squishing sound. "Come along, Shand. We've got work to do." In actual fact, his immediate plans did not include the young constable, but he wanted to spare him the ordeal of being ragged, or, rather more likely, congratulated by his colleagues for nearly drowning his superior.

When Powell arrived at the Salar Lodge, there was a message from Barrett waiting for him, indicating among other things that he would be arriving Saturday morning. It's about bloody time, Powell thought irritably. After a reviving soak in a near-scalding tub, he set off for the Ravenscroft Guesthouse.

Mrs. Blakey, a grandmotherly woman with a pleasant manner, ushered Powell into a sitting room chockablock with embroidered cushions of various shapes and sizes.

"I'll tell Mr. Sanders you're here," she said with a conspiratorial chuckle, still under the impression that she was presiding over some sort of joyous reunion.

When Sanders appeared a few minutes later it was obvious that he was not in the best of shape. Bleary eyed and even more tousled than usual, he collapsed into a chair and gestured for Powell to do likewise. His fingers quavered as he lit a cigarette.

"You'll have to excuse me. I haven't been getting much sleep lately."

A bit edgy, are we? Powell thought coldly. He was going to enjoy this.

"I've been expecting you, actually," Sanders continued. "As soon as I found out about Pinky I figured you'd come looking for me."

"Really? Now why would you think that?"

"I was the last person he was with, right?" He ran his

fingers through his hair. "Look, I want you to know that I consider Pinky to be my friend. I've known him only a short time, it's true, but we've become good chums all the same."

How touching. "It's odd that you haven't gone to visit your old chum in hospital, then."

"Yeah, well, I feel badly about that. I've called the hospital to see how he's getting on, of course, but under the circumstances I thought it best to keep a low profile."

"And just what circumstances are those, Mr. Sanders?"

Sanders smiled weakly. "*Mr.* Sanders, is it? As bad as all that?"

Powell did not reply.

Sanders shrugged. "Have it your way. Well, for starters, the rumor began to circulate that what happened to Pinky was no accident."

"Where did you hear that particular rumor?"

"Perhaps I should back up a bit. Pinky has probably told you that I left him fishing at the Old Bridge to run some errands in town. When I returned an hour later he was gone."

"What time was that?"

"Half-past three, give or take."

"Were you driving your Escort?"

"Yes."

"Go on."

"At first I thought that he must have wandered downstream to compare notes with the fellows on the next beat, but when I checked, there was no one there either. It seemed a bit strange at the time. On the way back I found Pinky's rod lying on the riverbank. At that point I really began to worry. When I checked in at the Salar Lodge to see if he was there, I bumped into old George Stuart, who wasted no time in telling me that someone had tried to drown Pinky. 'Just like Mr. Murray,' he said." Sanders looked sheepish. "To be completely honest, I panicked. I didn't want to get involved."

"Well, you are involved," Powell snapped. "In an investigation of attempted murder, and that's just for openers."

"What's that supposed to mean?" Sanders demanded, shifting nervously in his chair.

"According to Peter Grant, you purchased a new rod from him about a week ago. You then returned yesterday and bought another one, claiming to have broken the first. You were carrying the new one when we bumped into each other at the shop. I'd be very interested to learn what happened to that first rod of yours."

Sanders shook his head painfully. "It was a crazy thing to do, I'll admit it, but I've become kind of hooked on this salmon fishing, if you'll pardon the pun, and I wanted to try out my new rod. I wasn't able to get another ticket on the hotel water, so I decided to throw caution to the wind and have a go at Castle Glyn. I didn't think anybody would mind under the circumstances."

"With Charles Murray dead, you mean."

Sanders took a deep drag of his cigarette. "Yes."

Powell fixed him with a deceptively placid gaze. "You realize, of course, that poaching is against the law in this country. Frankly, I don't believe you're that stupid. Quite the contrary, I'd say."

"It's a minor offense, surely. Let's just say I made an error in judgment." Sanders met Powell's eyes with bloodshot intensity.

Powell smiled humorlessly. "But an error in judgment with potentially far-reaching consequences, wouldn't you agree?"

"What do you mean?"

"I'm given to understand that you're a freelance journalist, Mr. Sanders, and I expect you have to do a fair bit of traveling in your line of work. I shouldn't imagine you'd wish to be encumbered by a police record. The precise nature of the transgression, I think, is rather beside the point. The customs and immigration authorities don't usually split hairs over that sort of thing."

Sanders sighed heavily. "Okay, now that the cat's out of the bag I've got nothing to hide, and whether you believe it or not, I'd like nothing more than to see you nail the bastard who tried to kill Pinky." He leaned forward. "It's true that I'm a reporter. And as I'm sure you've already guessed, I came here to do a story on Charles Murray. It seems that the public never tires of that sort of crap—you know, a glimpse into the lives of the rich and famous. But it pays the bills."

"Perhaps we can discuss your journalistic integrity later. I'm still waiting to hear about your little poaching adventure."

Sanders indignantly drew on his cigarette. "I was caught in the act. Someone chucked a great bloody rock at me—I could have been killed!"

"Did you see who it was?"

He shook his head. "There was a shout and then a big splash. I assumed it was a gamekeeper or somebody like that, but I wasn't about to stick around to find out. I got the hell out of there as fast as I could. It was only later that I realized I'd lost my rod somewhere along the way.

I've been fretting ever since that somebody would find it and somehow trace it back to me."

Powell frowned. "I don't understand. Why didn't you just leave Kinlochy?"

Sanders smiled bitterly. "If I had, I guess I'd have saved myself a lot of trouble. The truth is I wanted to finish my story and to do that I needed to interview Heather Murray. Unfortunately, she seems immune to my charms and refuses to see me. But if nothing else, I'm a persistent son of a bitch. As a matter of fact, I called her again yesterday afternoon, but she'd have none of it. She even threatened to call the police. That was enough for me. I decided to leave well enough alone and was planning to return to London tonight. But now . . ." He shrugged.

"Exactly what line were you going to take in this story of yours?"

"A biographical sketch for starters—you know, local boy makes good, that sort of thing—a generous helping of Highland color, and then the *pièce de résistance*: a tantalizing suggestion that, despite his alleged retirement, Charles Murray was in fact working on a major new deal, possibly his biggest yet."

Powell perked up. "What gave you that idea?"

"I didn't have any hard evidence, really. Just a reporter's intuition. Plus the odd suggestive tidbit."

"Such as?"

"Well, for one thing I bumped into an old associate of his in the Grouse and Butt the other day. A well-known Vancouver stock promoter. I overheard him ordering a taxi for Castle Glyn."

"That wouldn't be Oliver Pickens, would it?"

Sanders looked mildly surprised. "You've been doing your homework, Chief Superintendent. I'm impressed."

"Do you remember what day it was you saw Pickens in the pub?"

"Let's see, I remember it was a couple of days after I'd arrived. I'd have to check my notes for the exact date."

"Do that."

Sanders rummaged through the pockets of his tweed jacket and produced a tatty black notebook similar to the one Powell himself carried. He smiled weakly. "I never go anywhere without it." He fumbled through the pages, tearing one or two in his haste. "Yes, here it is. It was the Friday before Murray was killed." He offered the open notebook to Powell.

Powell declined. "I'll take your word for it. Go on."

"I followed Pickens to Castle Glyn, hoping to catch them in the act, so to speak." He frowned. "I wasn't able to get past the butler, so I never did get to interview Murray—" He broke off thoughtfully.

"Did you have any other evidence that Murray was working on a new project?"

Sanders regarded Powell carefully before replying. "Like I said, it was just a hunch."

Time now, Powell thought, to flush out his quarry. "You mentioned earlier that you decided to go to ground when you heard about Pinky's mishap. Surely it must have occurred to you that you would only draw attention to yourself?"

Sanders yawned. "I had a story to finish, and the last thing I needed was to become embroiled in a police investigation. Ironic, isn't it?"

"If you say so." Now to let him have it with both barrels. "Let's return for a moment to your old chum Pinky. We know that he stumbled onto something at the Old Bridge. In fact, we think that was the reason someone tried to kill him."

"Oh, yes?" Sanders said warily.

"He found a fishing rod. Yours, I believe."

The color drained from Sanders's face. "Good God, you don't think I . . ." He hesitated, realization suddenly dawning on him. "Yes, I see now," he said quietly.

Powell leaned back comfortably in his chair. "You're a writer of sorts, Mr. Sanders. Why don't you and I plot a little detective story? Should be a piece of cake with all the material we've got to work with. Let's begin with a mild-mannered Canadian reporter who comes to Scotland to do a story about a wealthy compatriot living like a laird near a pleasant little Speyside town. To get things off to a good start, we'll bump this latter chap off in the first chapter.

"Our reporter, never one to miss a journalistic opportunity, decides to stay on to do a little poking around. Unfortunately, he gets involved in a bit of poaching on the deceased's estate and, for some strange reason apart from the obvious one, seems frightened half to death his little peccadillo will be discovered. That's when another character, a perfectly harmless chap, whom we shall have introduced previously, comes across some incriminating evidence, and our faithful scribe, fearing exposure, attempts to do him in. Which suggests perhaps that our hero is not so mild mannered after all." Powell paused, his brows furrowed in mock concentration. "Please don't hesitate to jump in with your ideas—we can sort of roundtable it. I'm not much good at this creative stuff."

Sanders sat motionless, his face a deathly pale. His eyes were fixed on Powell with morbid fascination.

"Writer's block, Mr. Sanders? I shouldn't worry, happens to the best of us. Now, where were we? Oh, yes. This next bit will require our utmost concentration. Our loyal readers will no doubt be wondering why our man would attempt to commit a murder simply to conceal a minor poaching offense. Doesn't make sense, does it? So just to ginger things up, let us suppose that our reporter had tried a little illicit fishing on the laird's water on one previous occasion—immediately prior to the murder, shall we say. We'll have an impeccably reliable witness place him at the scene, of course." He watched Sanders closely, knowing all too well that he was on a fishing expedition of his own.

For a few seconds Sanders seemed incapable of speaking, but eventually he managed to blurt out, "You must be mad!"

CHAPTER 14

The color began to return to Sanders's face, seemingly in direct proportion to his growing state of agitation. "I can't believe you're serious!"

"Oh, I'm deadly serious, Mr. Sanders. Let's look at the facts. A few hours before Charles Murray was murdered, I saw somebody fishing on the estate water. This person was fishing with a single-handed rod, just like the one you were using when I first met you two days later. There hasn't been another like it seen on the river since."

"I tell you it wasn't me!" Sanders protested vehemently. "You must believe me!"

"Where were you, then, last Monday evening around six?"

"How am I supposed to remember that?"

"I'd advise you to try."

Sanders picked up his notebook with trembling fingers and began to flip through it. Beads of perspiration had sprung from his brow. "Let's see—Monday—here it is. 'Toured Spey Valley.' For the first few days after I arrived I did the usual tourist bit to absorb some background atmosphere for my story."

"Not very specific, I'm afraid."

"I don't—wait a minute, I remember now! I visited the distillery at Glenlivet. I telephoned Mrs. Blakey from there to tell her I wouldn't be taking the evening meal at the guesthouse. On the way back I stopped for a bite to eat in a small village pub—for the life of me, I can't remember the name of the place—I suppose if I had a map . . ." He frowned and shook his head. "I don't remember exactly what time I got back, but I do remember that it was raining."

"May I see your notebook now?"

Sanders handed it over.

Powell leafed through it. After a few minutes he said, "I'll keep this, if you don't mind."

Sanders waved his hand in a gesture of acquiescence.

"I'm going to ask you to alter your travel plans for the time being, Mr. Sanders. I may need to talk to you again."

"Am I under arrest?"

"Not at the moment."

"But it amounts to the same thing."

"You're free to do whatever you wish. I'm simply asking that you delay your departure for a little while, that's all."

Sanders nodded wearily.

"Later today, another police officer will come to take a formal statement, which you will be asked to sign."

Sanders gazed blearily at Powell. "How long is this going to take?"

"That depends, doesn't it?"

* * *

PC Shand scratched his head. "I don't get it, Mr. Powell. Even if Sanders does turn out to be your mystery fisherman, it doesn't prove he's the murderer, does it?"

Powell sighed. "No. But I'm still convinced he isn't telling the whole story. For one thing, there's a marked change in the character of his notes over the period in question. Initially, the entries are very precise and detailed, as one might expect of a reporter's notes. After the murder, however, they become sketchy at best. Curious, don't you think?"

"Sir?"

"Murray's death presented Sanders with a golden journalistic opportunity. Yet, judging by his notes, he seems to have more or less lost interest in the subject, as if his work had already been completed."

"It does seem a bit odd, all right," Shand agreed.

There was a prolonged silence during which Powell was lost in thought.

"Is there anything I can do, sir?" Shand ventured hesitantly.

"Get over to the guesthouse and take a statement from him, and don't forget to caution him. I've made some notes you can use as a guide. And when you're done keep a discreet eye on him. We don't want him giving us the slip. And, oh, yes, get in touch with the Glenlivet distillery and see if they've any record of his visit. He may have signed the visitor's book or bought some product with a credit card. You can run out there to verify it if necessary. Right, off you go, then. And don't forget your swimming lesson."

When he was alone, it suddenly struck Powell that the

entire case revolved around various events that had occurred in the general vicinity of the Old Bridge: his sighting of the mysterious fisherman, the incident involving Arthur Ogden and John Sanders, Pinky's narrow scrape, and possibly even the murder itself. Once again, he had the rather disquieting sensation, which he was at a loss to explain, that he was overlooking something important.

Bob Whitely slewed the van around the graveled drive of Castle Glyn and skidded to an abrupt halt in front of the house. He leapt out and took the broad stone steps two at a time. Ross, caught completely off guard, was left stammering at the door long after Whitely had outflanked him. By the time the butler's atrophied synapses had caught up with events, there was only the faint slamming of a distant door to contend with.

"Och, well, who gives a damn," he muttered as he slowly closed the door, this being just the latest in a series of recent indignities.

Heather Murray looked up, startled, as the door flew open. "It's you," she said quietly. "I thought we'd agreed that you shouldn't come here."

"You know I can't stay away from you," Whitely said, approaching her. "Besides, I'm sick and tired of playing these little games."

He pulled her to him, but her body was limp, passive. Releasing her suddenly, he stepped back.

"What's the matter?" he asked sharply.

She turned away. "I don't know—it's still too soon. I need time to think."

He looked at her wildly. "What's there to think about? I love you. What else matters?"

"A lot has happened, Bob. You can't expect me to make up my mind now."

"Look, I'll come with you, if that's what you're worried about. There's nothing to keep me here. Dad's thinking about selling the hotel, so I'll have some money."

He waited for her to speak, hopefully at first and then with growing anger. Eventually she turned to face him. Her expression told him everything he needed to know.

"You bloody bitch!" he hissed, moving toward her.

It seemed to Powell that Nigel had aged perceptibly over the past week and a half. He stood bent over the kitchen counter, his long face pale and unshaven. He glanced up, expressionless, when he heard his name.

"Do you mind if I carry on with this?" He gestured vaguely with the long, thin knife he was using to carve a rare joint of beef, left over from dinner and destined for tomorrow's sandwiches, Powell surmised.

"Of course not." Powell noticed that a trickle of red juice was dripping from the edge of the cutting board and splattering rather alarmingly on the white tile floor. "Something's come up, Nigel. I need to talk to you."

"More questions?" Whitely seemed strangely passive, as if resigned to whatever fate had in store for him.

"I'm afraid so. I need to know where you were yesterday afternoon from about half-past one to half-past three."

There was a slight hesitation in the motion of the knife. "Let me see—I helped Ruby with the lunch things and then I went out to run some errands. It must have been around two-thirty when I left the hotel."

"Did you take the van?"

Whitely shot Powell a glance. "No, I borrowed Ruby's Mini."

"Why?"

"Bob had taken the van to pick up a load of bricks for the garden wall."

"What time did you get back?"

"It was four-thirty. I remember checking my watch as I pulled into the car park. I had a few things I needed to do before dinner and I didn't want to cut it too fine."

"Go on."

Nigel seemed momentarily nonplussed. "I—I came into the hotel, and it was then that Ruby told me about Mr. Warburton's accident." He looked up at Powell, a faint flicker of concern in his expression. "How is Mr. Warburton?"

"As well as can be expected under the circumstances," Powell replied gravely. He neglected to mention that Pinky was to be discharged tomorrow. "Nigel, why did you go to the Old Bridge yesterday afternoon?"

There was an awkward silence.

Eventually Nigel spoke. "I wanted to speak to Mr. Warburton."

"What about?"

"Business, actually. I knew that Mr. Warburton was an estate agent."

"Oh, yes?"

"I wanted to ask him about the Salar Lodge." He took a halting breath. "To see how much the old place would fetch nowadays."

The quaver in Nigel's voice spoke volumes. The lean years laboring at Maggie's side to build up their business, the lingering emptiness following her death, and, more recently, the nagging doubts about Bob. But Powell knew that anything he could say of a personal nature would only make things worse for the both of them.

"What happened?" he prompted gently.

"I wasn't able to speak to Mr. Warburton." As if to answer Powell's unspoken question, he continued mechanically, "There was somebody else there—parked by Mr. Warburton's Land Rover. I wanted to speak to him in private, you understand, so I turned around and came back to the hotel."

"The other vehicle, can you describe it?"

Whitely looked forlornly at Powell. "It was the van," he said slowly.

"Yours?"

He nodded.

"What time was it, Nigel? Think carefully—it's important."

"It must have been a little before three."

"Do you have any idea what Bob was doing there?"

"No."

"Didn't you think to ask him afterward?"

"Why should I have? It didn't seem important at the time." There was a tremor in his voice.

"Nigel, at approximately three yesterday afternoon, someone tried to kill Mr. Warburton."

Nigel seemed to hunch even farther over the cutting board and did not speak for some time. Finally, he said in a barely audible voice, "There was some idle talk, of course, because of what happened to Mr. Murray." He shook his head slowly. "But it's just not possible."

"Nigel, I think there *is* a connection between what happened to Mr. Warburton and Charles Murray's murder."

Whitely whirled around with startling animation. "Surely you're not suggesting that my Bob had anything to do with either?"

"I'm not suggesting anything, Nigel."

Whitely seemed bewildered. "It's just that—I don't know—all these questions."

"I'm only trying to sort it all out. And I know you wouldn't want to leave a shadow hanging over Bob." Powell suppressed a stab of guilt.

Nigel sighed wearily. "How can I help?"

"Why don't you begin by telling me about Bob and Heather Murray."

Nigel examined his knife with studied concentration. "She and her father stayed at the hotel for a few days when they first arrived in Kinlochy. Bob took a fancy to her right from the start, and they soon became fairly serious. At first Mr. Murray seemed pleased enough and even encouraged them. He seemed happy that Heather was making friends. But then he changed. He became increasingly reclusive, hardly ever leaving Castle Glyn. And his attitude toward Heather became what I can only describe as overprotective. At one point he even accused Bob of gold digging—those were his exact words! A ridiculous suggestion! Bob was head over heels in love with the lass, or I don't know my own son."

"Was?"

"They called it off a few months ago. It was Heather's decision, although Bob has never said much about it. It's strange, though. The lass has a mind of her own and I can't imagine her being pressured to do anything against her will, even by her own father." He sighed. "I don't know, perhaps the strain just proved to be too much for her."

"Can you explain Murray's change of heart?"

He shrugged, "It's hard to say. He lost his wife some years back and took it rather hard, I understand." He paused reflectively for a moment, his thoughts transparent. "Perhaps after retiring he had too much time on his hands. He didn't seem to mix much with the local folk, but some of them can be a bit clannish when it comes to outsiders."

"So you don't think it was anything in particular?"

"Personal, you mean?"

"Yes."

"I don't see how it could have been. I've tried to broach the subject with Bob but, well, you know this younger generation as well as I do, Mr. Powell. Besides, the lad's got a lot on his mind," he ventured hopefully, as if that might explain everything.

"How did Bob take it?"

"Pretty hard, I think. As I did. I was hoping he might settle down and—but it doesn't matter now, does it?"

"Nigel, I know that Charles Murray was at the hotel on the night he was killed . . ." He left it hanging.

Whitely turned slowly to face Powell. He spoke quietly and deliberately. "He threatened me, Mr. Powell. He told me that if I didn't keep my son away from his daughter, he'd withdraw the hotel's fishing rights."

"Could he have done that? Surely there's a contract of some sort?"

Whitely nodded. "The lease contains a clause that provides for the termination of the agreement at any time. With the stroke of a pen he could have destroyed everything Maggie and I've built here. You might be surprised to learn that the Salar Lodge provides us a living, but not much more. Without the fishing I'd be finished. I pleaded with him to be reasonable, but he just laughed. I hated him then. Now it just seems pathetic."

"Had he made similar threats before?"

Whitely shook his head.

"I don't understand, Nigel. You say Bob and Heather had stopped seeing each other months ago. Why would Murray wait until now to deliver his ultimatum?"

"I haven't a clue, Mr. Powell."

"Did you mention the incident to Bob?"

"Like I said, I didn't want to worry him."

"Do you recall what time it was when Murray left the hotel?"

Whitely knit his brow. "Let's see. It was just before Ruby got back from her meeting. She usually gets in around eleven, so it must have been around ten-thirty."

"What did you do after he'd gone?"

"I waited up for Ruby and then turned in." There was a lengthy pause. "Mr. Powell, I . . ." He wiped his forehead with a juice-stained hand, leaving a lurid smudge behind. "I know my Bob has got a bit of a temper, always has, but he would never hurt anyone, I know he wouldn't." He blinked moistly.

"I'm sure you're right, Nigel," Powell said, trying to convey a sense of reassurance he did not feel.

It was obvious, Powell reflected the next morning as he searched for a convenient vantage point overlooking the Old Bridge, that Nigel was worried sick about Bob. But whether he could actually bring himself at a conscious level to suspect his son of killing Charles Murray was another matter. The lad had at least two plausible motives. One was obvious: to remove the obstacle standing between himself and Heather Murray, with all that implied both romantically and financially. The other possibility was more problematic. Bob may have felt the need to protect his father from ruin at the hands of Charles Murray. Only there was no evidence Bob had even been aware of Murray's threat against his father until Powell, himself, had mentioned it at the hill loch. And if young Whitely had in fact been in Aberdeen on the night in question, it should be easy enough to corroborate. The lad had supposedly been looking for a job; he must have talked to someone. Powell tried to sweep the implications of this line of inquiry from his already cluttered mind.

He sat down on a grassy knoll and took in the view. Below and slightly upstream of his position was the graceful stone arch of the Old Bridge. Immediately downstream of the bridge he could just make out Pinky's rock, as he now thought of it. Sunlight sparkled off the riffles separating the curving blue pools of the Spey, and across the river, set amidst its green lawns like a golden crown in a baize-lined case, was Castle Glyn. Powell found himself thinking about Heather Murray again.

He shook his head irritably and began to work through the thing once more. What bothered him most was the attempt on Pinky's life. He felt—irrationally, he knew—that somehow he should have been able to forestall events. But the more he thought about it, the less sense it all made. Even if Sanders had succeeded in preventing the fishing rod from coming to light, it had been a tremendous risk to take, with nothing really to gain. Ironically, the attempt on Pinky's life had turned out to be the very thing that had implicated the Canadian, which could hardly have been the point. Or could it?

Powell's mind began to race wildly. Could someone have tried to kill Pinky simply to lay a false scent, to point the finger at Sanders? It seemed preposterous. Which raised another, even more unsettling possibility. What if the two crimes were not related in the way that he had assumed? Or not related at all?

Powell had always accepted as an article of faith that the detection of crime was essentially a rational process and that, given enough time and dogged persistence, even the most intractable puzzles could eventually be untangled. The problem arose with random or fortuitous crimes of the night stalker variety, when the killer had no particular relationship with the victim. For a whimsical moment he imagined that a crazed anti-blood-sport fanatic was running amok on the Spey, preying on unsuspecting fisherman to avenge the coldblooded murder of countless thousands of salmon over the years.

He was jarred back to reality by a dissonant droning, which had begun to reverberate amongst the hills. It took him a second to recognize the racket for what it was.

"Bagpipes! Bloody hell!" he said aloud.

The wailing cacophony sounded a harsh, albeit strangely familiar, note amidst the hitherto vast silence. Powell recalled the English canard that the Scots' long history of suicidal charges on the battlefield could be ascribed solely to a frenzied desire to escape the skirling pipes. Then he suddenly remembered where he had heard the sound before—yesterday morning, just before he'd been dragged half drowned from the river by McInnes. At the time it had seemed in his sodden and desperate state like a hallucination. But now he recalled Ogden's account of a similar experience, which hadn't until that moment seemed important.

His eyes scanned the scrubby hillside, which dropped in steep, broken slabs to the river, but he could see nothing out of the ordinary. He scrambled to his feet and set off down a well-tramped deer path toward the only piece of cover that seemed sufficient to conceal a piper, kilt, and a set of bagpipes: a rocky prominence rising a couple of hundred yards away like a gray sail above a blue-green sea of juniper. But before he got very far the piping stopped as suddenly as it had begun. Feeling exposed, he picked up the pace. When he was within a hundred feet of his objective, which at close view turned out to be a steep pile of blocky rubble, he slowed and covered the intervening ground as stealthily as he could. Except for the rustling of his own passage, there was not a sound. Perhaps he'd been mistaken about the source; he knew from his climbing days that the hills could be deceiving.

He crept round the base of the rock. Nothing. He paused to consider the situation. A trickle of fine gravel whispered somewhere above him.

Before he could react, he was startled by a rough voice, "Say your prayers, laddie."

He looked up slowly, heart pounding, into the mindless, binocular gape of a twelve-bore shotgun.

CHAPTER 15

"Mr. Powell, sir! W-what are you doing here?" George Stuart, dressed in full Highland regalia, lowered his gun, instinctively breaking open the action.

"I could ask you the same question," Powell snapped, struggling mightily to regain his dignity.

"Well, sir," Stuart said awkwardly, loosening his collar with a thick finger, "I just came up here to play a little, er, tune." He gestured at the bagpipes lying in a heap like some supine tartan sheep, legs erect, on the ledge beside him.

"Come down from there, George," Powell ordered. "Quite frankly, the view from here leaves a lot to be desired."

The Scot flushed pinkly. He handed down the gun, smoothed his kilt, and climbed demurely down.

"Now then, what's this all about?" Powell asked sternly.

Stuart stood to attention. "Well, sir, when the laird has died it is customary amongst the Stuarts to sound the family lament every morning at sunrise for not less than twenty-one days."

191

Powell raised a skeptical eyebrow. "Charles Murray wasn't exactly chief of the clan, George."

"Nevertheless, sir," Stuart said with great dignity, "I feel it's my duty. I spent many a good year in the employ of the estate."

"That doesn't explain the gun."

"Well, sir, what wi' reports of poachers about and after what happened to Mr. Warburton, a man canna be too careful."

"That's what the police are for, George."

Stuart looked like a chastened puppy. "I'm truly sorry, Mr. Powell." Then he brightened and reached into his jacket. "Here, this'll fix you up proper." He handed Powell an engraved sterling flask. "It's a private bottling of Glen Callum, put up in Edinburgh. My brother-in-law knows the merchant."

A few minutes later things were looking considerably brighter. Powell questioned Stuart closely and confirmed that the Salar Lodge's bartender had in fact been performing the Stuart lament from the same rocky prominence every morning since the discovery of Murray's body. He normally piped at dawn when most self-respecting fishermen were still abed, which no doubt explained why he hadn't been reported more frequently. But on a few occasions, including the previous morning, he'd been a little late getting started. Powell looked around. The rocks commanded a clear view of the bridge and its various approaches: the road to Kinlochy, the river path, and, on the far bank, the road to Dulnay Bridge and the steep track descending to the river from Castle Glyn. It occurred to him that George might well have noticed some interesting comings and goings during his daily sojourn.

At first Stuart seemed slightly puzzled by Powell's question. Powell explained patiently, "We're investigating a murder and an attempted murder. The thing is, we're interested in anything out of the ordinary, anything at all that might suggest a line of inquiry."

Stuart scratched his stubbly chin. "I'm sorry, Mr. Powell." He adjusted his spectacles. "These old peepers aren't what they used to be."

"What about yesterday morning?" said Powell, hope fading fast.

"Well, there did seem to be a wee commotion down at the Old Bridge—swarming around like ants they was—but I couldna make it oot."

Powell sighed. "Tell me, George, what do you think about this business? About Mr. Murray, I mean."

"Well, sir, I didna know him that well. I spoke wi' him a few times when he and Miss Murray was staying at the hotel, mostly about sport, ye ken."

"How did he strike you?"

"He seemed a pleasant enough sort. And it's to his credit he kept auld Ross on."

"What do you mean?"

"Donald Ross has been plowterin' aboot Castle Glyn for longer than I can remember. You might say he just comes wi' the house. Mr. Murray could have let him go, but according to Miss Morrow, the housemaid, he didna have the heart."

"What about Miss Murray?"

George shrugged. "Much like her father, I'd say."

"Oh, really?" Powell was mildly surprised.

"Aye, reserved, like."

"I've heard that young Mr. Whitely had been courting Miss Murray. Is that true?"

"It's no' a secret."

"I understand that Mr. Murray was none too pleased about it."

"I wouldna know about that, Mr. Powell."

"I've also heard they stopped seeing each other some time ago."

"Aye, that's true, I believe."

"Do you have any idea why they broke it off?"

Stuart shrugged unconvincingly.

Powell sighed, exasperated. "Look, George, I can ask for an official statement, if you'd prefer. But I need to know the truth; the lives of innocent people may depend upon it." Melodramatic, but effective, judging by Stuart's reaction.

"Well, to tell the truth, Mr. Powell, they used to argy-bargy like cats and dogs. Terrible spats they had. I over-heard them once when I was cleaning up behind the bar and another time in the hotel car park." He shifted on his feet uncomfortably. "Then they'd kiss and make up, sweet as you please and other sich foolishness," he added reprovingly.

"Do you know what Nigel thought about it?"

"He never confided in me, of course. But I got the impression it upset him, especially when they finally went their separate ways."

"What about Ruby?"

"She took it pretty hard. But then she's always treated young Mr. Whitely like the son she never had." Stuart snorted and spat. "I know it's not my place to say so, Mr.

Powell, but as far as I'm concerned, that laddie's a right scunner."

"Whatever do you mean, George?"

"You dinna really know him. Sure he's charmin' as you please with the guests—butter wouldn't melt in his mouth. But he carries on like Lord Muck wi' the rest of us. Thinks because he went to school down south he's better than ordinary folk. Spoiled rotten if you ask me. And there's somethin' else—" He stopped abruptly, as if suddenly realizing that he was on the brink of going too far.

"Yes?"

Stuart drew a deep breath. "There was a chambermaid used to work at the hotel, Mary MacLean—perhaps you remember her? A soft-spoken lass with lovely red hair? It was a few years back now." He shifted from one foot to the other. "There was talk going around that young Mr. Whitely had, er—" he blushed profusely "—taken advantage of the lass. There was never any complaint from her, mind you, but one mornin' she was gone, without even giving her notice. Very peculiar if you ask me."

Powell wondered what he was driving at, but decided not to press the point. At least not now. "You know how unreliable gossip can be, George," he said pointedly.

Stuart's jaw was set stubbornly. "That's as may be, Mr. Powell, but I ken what I ken."

When Powell got back to the Salar Lodge he telephoned Detective-Sergeant Black in London. He was disappointed, but not surprised, to learn that Pickens was sticking to his story. After lunch Powell drove to the hospital and collected Pinky, who from all appearances had fully recovered from his ordeal. On the way back to Kinlochy, Warburton listened attentively while Powell gave his account of the interview with John Sanders.

Pinky seemed pleased with himself. "You will be interested to know that John came to see me last night. He was most contrite for not having come earlier. He explained everything. I pride myself in being an excellent judge of character, Erskine, and I simply refuse to believe that John had anything to do with this business."

"I'm not prepared to rule anything out at this point."

Pinky cleared his throat nervously. "I don't know quite how to put this, old man, but do you think there's any danger of a repeat performance?"

"I think it's highly unlikely. But just to be on the safe side, I want you on the London train tomorrow afternoon; I'll sleep more easily with you safely out of the way."

Warburton nodded.

"In the meantime, I'd like you to stick close to the Salar Lodge. I'll leave Shand to keep an eye on you."

Warburton smiled. "My own personal bodyguard?"

"Something like that." Powell regarded his friend with mixed emotions. He had invited Pinky to Kinlochy for a bit of rest and relaxation, but it hadn't exactly worked out that way. For either of them, come to that. He could not dispel the growing feeling that, like a river tumbling headlong to the sea, events were unfolding beyond his control, which was hardly reassuring under the circumstances. His fatalistic musings were interrupted by Warburton.

"What about this Pickens chap? It seems to me from what you've said that he had as good a reason as anyone to settle scores with Murray."

"Perhaps. But someone tried to drown you, Pinky, and of one thing I'm absolutely certain: It wasn't Oliver Pickens. I'm still convinced that there's a connection between what happened to you and the murder of Charles Murray, although for the life of me I can't put my finger on it. I keep coming back to that damned fishing rod and running up against the same brick wall. But you can chalk up another thing I'm certain of: John Sanders's reason for coming to Kinlochy had absolutely nothing to do with journalistic curiosity."

"What do you mean?"

Powell explained about the notebook.

Warburton frowned. "There must be somebody else—somebody who would have benefited from Murray's death."

Powell sighed heavily. "I can tell you this much, Pinky—there is no shortage of possibilities."

Powell experienced a growing sense of ambivalence as he mounted the steps of Castle Glyn. He had put it off as long as possible, for reasons which, even now, he remained unwilling to consciously confront. The door opened to reveal Ross, no sign of recognition in his rheumy eyes. He tottered aside muttering to himself, having resigned himself by now to the continual invasion of Castle Glyn by riffraff of all descriptions.

When Powell entered the sitting room, Heather Murray, who was standing in front of the fireplace, turned quickly away.

"You might have called first," she said.

Powell felt a tightening in the pit of his stomach. "Look at me, Miss Murray."

She turned around to face him. In ghastly contrast to her pale complexion, a livid bluish yellow bruise extended from her left eye to her cheekbone. Her eyes blazed defiantly. Powell looked at her in silence for a moment, buffeted by a storm of conflicting emotions. When he spoke his voice was taut. "Who did this to you?"

She did not answer.

"It was Bob Whitely, wasn't it?"

She turned away again, reaching for a cigarette on the mantelshelf. Before Powell could react, she'd lit it with a tiny gold lighter. She inhaled deeply. "Does it really matter?"

"It matters to me. Assault is against the law in this country."

"An eye for an eye, is that it?"

"If you like. See here, Miss Murray, I'm not interested in debating the ethical basis of the criminal justice system. I'm just trying to do my bloody job. Now, I'll ask you again: Who did this to you?"

"That's my business, until I decide otherwise."

"I know all about you and Bob Whitely." He could see her shoulders tighten. He pressed on. "I think your father approved at first. He was probably pleased that you'd begun to make a life for yourself here. But it wasn't long before he became concerned about the relationship. Not to put too fine a point on it, Miss Murray, it's no secret that young Whitely has an extremely volatile nature. I don't believe he'd physically abused you at that point, but the tendency was there, nonetheless. I think your father could see it, which is why he wanted you to end the relationship."

She turned and regarded him steadily, her eyes like cool, emerald pools. "You're very perceptive, Mr. Powell."

Powell could detect neither sincerity nor sarcasm in her voice, nor anything else for that matter. "You've stated to both Mr. Barrett and myself that you'd spent the weekend in question with a friend. You were with Bob, weren't you?"

She slipped lightly into a chair, drawing her legs under her. "Yes, it's true."

Powell felt a twinge of guilt. "I know this must be difficult for you, Miss Murray, but it is necessary, I'm afraid." Marvelous things, cliches. "Would you like to tell me about it?"

She brushed a strand of hair from her forehead. "Everything I told you before was true. I just left out the part about Bob. It's rather ironic. We hadn't seen each other for months. Then about three weeks ago he called me. He'd apparently heard a rumor that Castle Glyn was to be put up for sale. He asked me what I was going to do. I told him that I hadn't decided, although in reality I'd already made up my mind to return to Canada with Father. Bob pleaded with me to stay. He promised to be more reasonable about things, so I agreed to go away with him for the weekend. To try to sort things out once and for all. I felt I owed him that much."

"I'm a little confused," Powell interjected in spite of himself. "You say your relationship with young Whitely had ended some months ago, yet you decided to spend the weekend with him?"

"We're being a little judgmental aren't we, Chief Superintendent?"

"Not at all," Powell lied. "I'm just trying to understand the nature of your relationship."

"Then I'll make it easy for you. We were lovers. It just didn't work out, that's all. Bob has more than his share of problems, and he needed more from me than I was able to give him. I wasn't prepared to be his lover, nursemaid, and surrogate mother. It's true that my father didn't like him, but in spite of what you may have heard, the decision to end the affair was mine. It's as simple as that."

"Not quite that simple, Miss Murray, surely."

"What do you mean?" Involuntarily, she touched her cheek.

"Do you know that Bob blamed your father for the breakup?"

She shrugged. "That doesn't surprise me."

"And are you aware that your father went to the Salar Lodge the night he was murdered and threatened to put Nigel Whitely out of business if he didn't keep Bob away from you?"

She seemed to grow even paler. "I—I'd told Father about going away with Bob to Pitlochry. He was livid of course, but I believe in being honest with people, Mr. Powell, don't you?" Her eyes searched his.

Powell thought it best not to answer.

"If I'd thought . . . but it doesn't matter now, does it?"

"You've said that you returned to Castle Glyn on Monday evening, but Bob didn't get back until the following morning. Where was he?"

"We'd originally planned to come back on Sunday, but I decided to stay an extra day and take in a play at the festival. Bob went on to Aberdeen Sunday afternoon."

"Do you know why?"

"He said he was going to look for a job."

"Just like that, a bolt out of the blue?"

"Look, Mr. Powell, I'd made it clear to Bob that it was over as far as I was concerned, but he seemed unable, or unwilling, to accept it. Perhaps a stint on an oil rig seemed a little like joining the Foreign Legion. You know, to forget." Was there a hint of self-mockery in her voice?

Curiously detached, Powell marveled at the inevitability of it all. Questions and answers, like those little Russian dolls, one within the other. "How is it then, Miss Murray, if it was all over, as you say, that you and Bob were seen together in Kinlochy less than a week after your father's death?"

At first she did not reply. When she did, she seemed more disappointed in him than anything else. "After my father's death, Bob paid the obligatory visit to Castle Glyn. It was all very proper, I can assure you. Then a few days later I happened to meet him in the High Street." She paused. "On that particular day I was feeling—well, not exactly on top of things. Perhaps vulnerable is a better word. Women are supposed to feel vulnerable, aren't they, Mr. Powell? It was a mistake, I can see that now. He probably thought I was leading him on."

Powell noticed that she had begun to tremble slightly, but he resisted the temptation to go to her. He felt faintly irrelevant.

"What are you going to do?" she asked eventually.

"Are you willing to bring forward a complaint?"

"Have you thought about Nigel?"

"That's not a consideration."

"Isn't it? It would probably kill him."

"You're aware that he'll probably do it again—to somebody else? They always do, you know."

"Perhaps he needs help then, not a jail sentence."

Powell experienced an all too familiar sense of frustration. He often got into similar debates with his sons. "It's your decision, of course," he said stiffly. "You know how to reach me if you change your mind."

"Right now, I just want to put this sordid little chapter of my life behind me. Now, if there's nothing else . . ."

"I assume that you stand to inherit your father's estate."

"Yes." She appraised him cooly.

"Did Bob know?"

"He probably guessed, don't you think?"

"Miss Murray, I want you to consider my next question very carefully before answering. Do you think Bob Whitely is capable of murder?"

She hesitated for a moment. "If you'd asked me before, I'd have thought it a ludicrous suggestion. Now, I'd have to say I—I just don't know."

Powell wondered as he drove back to Kinlochy what in God's name he was going to do.

CHAPTER 16

Barrett arrived on schedule the following morning. He and Powell conferred in the dining room over coffee.

"Where's Pinky?" Barrett asked.

"Out for a stroll with Shand, I expect."

Barrett stirred his coffee interminably with an irritating clinking of spoon against Spode. "While you were languishing here Speyside," he said when he was satisfied with the result, "I managed to dig up a few interesting tidbits."

"Such as?"

"To start with, it seems our friend Sanders is not only a reporter, but a reporter specializing in financial matters. He used to be business editor for the *Vancouver Sun* before he turned to freelancing."

"That explains quite a lot."

"And there's this." He casually tossed over a thick brown envelope. "It just so happens I have a contact at Mountie Headquarters in Ottawa with whom I've consulted on a number of previous occasions. I explained our problem and he was able to get a warrant."

The envelope was labeled BRITISH COLUMBIA SECURITIES COMMISSION. Powell extracted the contents of the envelope and quickly leafed through the pages. It was a veritable gold mine of information. For each brokerage house there was a printout of the account statements of clients with short positions for the companies of interest. It took him a few minutes to find what he was looking for. Under the heading WESTERN SECURITIES LTD., 1659 HOWE STREET, VANCOUVER, B. C. was the following entry:

JOHN G. SANDERS
ACCOUNT # 3051-35   MARGIN SHORT   BROKER 58

09/21/94	Westgold Mines, Inc.	76,500 S
11/09/94	Int'l., Silverload Ltd.	50,000 S
12/29/94	Aurora Mining Corp.	5,000 S
08/02/95	Cons. Grizzly Gold Ltd.	65,000 S

CASH BALANCE: $449,625   DATE: 03/31/96

"What does it mean?" Barrett said.

"In a nutshell, Sanders sold something he didn't own in order to make a profit."

"Sorry I asked."

Powell did his best to explain.

"Forgive me, Erskine, but so what?"

"I should have thought it was obvious. Sanders was in a position to profit handsomely when the prices of these shares fell on the news of Charles Murray's death. As I understand it the indicated cash balance of nearly four hundred fifty thousand dollars represents the proceeds of his short sales. If the value of the shares were to fall by, say, fifty percent, his profit after he covered his positions, that is after he bought the shares back, would be about two hundred twenty-five thousand dollars, less commissions. A tidy sum in anyone's book."

"Hmm." Barrett examined the entries with renewed interest. "But does it not strike you as curious that these, um, positions, as you call them, were established some time ago? Why would he wait so long to act?"

Powell shrugged. "I'll put the question to Paul Ritchie in London. And we'll need to have your Mountie friend contact Sanders's broker in Vancouver to see if he's done any trading since Murray's death."

Barrett leapt to his feet. "Consider it done. Now let's have a shufty around the Old Bridge."

Powell regarded his uneaten scone forlornly. "McInnes and his men have already gone over the area with a fine-tooth comb," he protested.

"Erskine, one can never be too thorough."

Powell knew better than to argue.

Later that morning Powell rang up Paul Ritchie in London, hoping he'd be in the office on a Saturday.

"Chief Superintendent, this is an unexpected pleasure. How goes the battle?" Ritchie went on to explain that he often came in on weekends to catch up on his paperwork—free from distractions.

Powell found it hard to imagine the broker without a phone in each ear and an eye on his quotation machine. "We have a few leads. That's why I'm calling. We've turned up a possible suspect who, interestingly enough, has been an active short seller of the shares of several of

Murray's companies." Powell recited the entries in Sanders's brokerage account statement.

"Interesting, but hardly conclusive. After all, your chap would not have been alone in his skepticism about the prospects of many of these companies. I can only assume that you have other reasons for your interest in this fellow."

"You've missed your calling, Mr. Ritchie. But please bear with me for a moment. It strikes me that these transactions were made over a year ago. If the idea was to kill Murray and then reap the rewards when the share prices collapsed, can you think of any reason why he'd wait so long to act? It seems to me that by delaying he'd run the risk of the share prices going up."

"Quite right, Chief Superintendent, because that's exactly what did happen and no one could have predicted it. You see, gold shares generally track the price of gold bullion, and since 1980 when the price peaked at eight hundred forty-three U.S. dollars an ounce, gold has been in an extended consolidation phase. And until quite recently, the junior resource markets have been in decline. But Charles had an uncanny knack for swimming against the tide. His last promotion is a case in point."

"What do you mean?"

"Early last year one of his smaller exploration companies, Grizzly Gold, made a discovery in Mexico—not significant enough to justify the subsequent rise in the price of the stock, but promising nonetheless. A fortuitous rally in the price of gold, coupled with Charles's undisputed promotional abilities, enabled him to capitalize on the situation. The other companies in Charles's stable were pulled along on Grizzly's coattails.

"Even after Charles retired, the stock continued to do well in anticipation of more positive results from the property. There's a major new drill program planned for this summer, as a matter of fact. The short sellers were no doubt getting squeezed, so, for them, the recent setback would've been something of a godsend."

"Can you think of any other reason for the increase in the share prices, something happening behind the scenes, perhaps?"

"Nothing official. Securities regulations require the disclosure of any change in material facts that might affect the price of a company's shares. But there are always rumors, of course."

"Rumors?"

"There was speculation a few months ago about the possibility of Grizzly being taken over by a major, but nothing ever came of it."

"A major?"

"A large mining company." Ritchie paused. "There is also talk of a joint venture between Grizzly and one of the other companies in the stable."

"I see. Tell me, Mr. Ritchie, if you were one of those short sellers, what would you have done in light of recent events?"

"I'd have begun to cover my positions last week when the share prices started to rally. But getting back to this fellow you're interested in, even if his timing had been perfect and he'd managed to cover at the lows, he'd have done well to break even."

"What do you mean?"

"Despite the decline after Charles's death, don't forget that the share prices had already increased substantially since the short positions in question were established. Furthermore, without getting into the intricacies of margin accounts, a good portion of the balance in the account represents money the client had to put up himself to cover potential losses when the market went against him. I'm just checking the charts and doing a rough calculation . . ."

Powell waited impatiently. He could hear the rustling of paper in the background.

"I was right," Ritchie said presently. "In fact he would have ended up slightly in the red."

"But better a small loss than a big one," Powell commented.

"That goes without saying, Chief Superintendent."

"I've been wondering about something . . ."

"Yes?"

"Why do you suppose Murray retired?"

There was a slight hesitation. "Difficult to say, really."

"He was apparently doing well with his latest promotion, yet I recall his daughter hinting that he'd been more or less forced to step aside," Powell continued. "You wouldn't happen to know anything about that?"

"These things happen in the business, Chief Superintendent."

"I see. Thank you, Mr. Ritchie. I won't take any more of your time. Once again you've been most helpful."

"Not at all, Chief Superintendent."

After ringing off, Ritchie sat for several minutes staring at the blank monitor of his desktop computer terminal. Almost imperceptibly, his expression tightened into a frown.

*   *   *

After a hurried conference with Barrett, Powell rang up Shand and issued some brief instructions.

When Powell and Barrett arrived at the Kinlochy police station fifteen minutes later, John Sanders was seated in the tiny office looking distinctly ill at ease, while Constable Shand busied himself fixing tea.

"Good afternoon, Mr. Sanders," Powell said heartily. "Tea? No? Well, you won't mind if Mr. Barrett and I partake. Many thanks, Shand." He took a soothing sip.

Shand couldn't help wondering about Chief Superintendent Powell's uncharacteristic ebullience, coupled with the fact that Chief Inspector Barrett seemed oddly restrained.

"I'd like you to have a look at this," Powell said. He removed a sheet of paper from his pocket, unfolded it, and handed it to Sanders.

The Canadian stared at one particular entry outlined with a red circle.

"The choice of ink was purely fortuitous, I can assure you," Powell remarked breezily.

Sanders looked blankly at Powell. "Where did you get this?"

"It's all perfectly legal, I can assure you."

Sanders's expression tightened. "Look here," he protested halfheartedly, "this is an invasion of privacy."

"That's as may be, Mr. Sanders. But this is a murder investigation, in case you'd forgotten." Powell reached out and retrieved the paper without encountering any resistance. "Do you have anything to say?"

"What the hell is this all about?"

Ignoring him, Powell turned to Barrett. "You know

what strikes me about Mr. Sanders's share portfolio, Alex?"

Barrett stirred languidly. "Pray tell."

"I'd say that he's got all his eggs in one basket. Golden eggs, at that. And in this case they're worth more with the goose dead."

"What are you driving at?" Sanders asked sharply.

"Only that you stood to benefit from Charles Murray's death."

Sanders buried his face in his hands and moaned. "Oh, God! It's not what you think."

"Let me tell you what I think. Over the past two years you've aggressively sold short the shares of various resource companies in which Charles Murray was involved. When you'd built up your positions you followed Murray over here on the pretext of doing a story on him, and then, when the opportunity presented itself, you killed him."

"No!" Sanders whispered.

"And when Pinky stumbled onto something that might link you with Murray," Powell persisted relentlessly, "you tried to kill *him* as well."

Sanders looked helplessly at Barrett, his emotions seemingly stretched to the breaking point. "It's not true! You must believe me!"

Barrett yawned. "You'd better come clean, then, hadn't you?"

Sanders ran his fingers through his unkempt hair. "I think I'll have that cup of tea, after all."

Barrett gestured to Shand, who obliged with a discreet absence of commotion.

The cup and saucer clattered loudly in Sanders's hand.

He recoiled with a look of alarm, spilling half the tea in the process.

"Get Mr. Sanders a napkin, will you, Shand?"

Sanders brushed frantically at his jacket. "I'm sorry— I—" He checked himself, set the cup down carefully, and took a steadying breath. "Look," he said, "this is ridiculous. You've actually got me believing that I've done something wrong."

"But you have, Mr. Sanders; you've already admitted it."

Sanders looked exasperated. "I don't mean the poaching. Look, I'll admit there's a grain of truth in what you've said, but you're dead wrong about Murray and Pinky. And Erskine, it's John, please. At least give me that."

Powell experienced a growing sense of apprehension as Sanders continued.

"You probably know by now that I used to be the business editor for a Vancouver daily. In the natural course of things I became involved in various penny stock promotions. You know how it is. You begin to think you're smarter than everyone else—that you can beat the market. Well, to cut a long story short, I got in over my head."

Powell shook his head. It didn't ring true. "Surely, having covered the scene as a journalist, you'd know better."

Sanders smiled thinly. "That's exactly the point. The majority of companies listed on junior stock exchanges represent nothing more than pipe dreams. They are, in effect, diminishing assets. Once the original premise of the venture proves untenable and the promoters bail out, the shares become so much worthless paper. It's unavoidable, really; it's simply the way venture capital markets work. It's no different than scientific research, or evolution, for that matter. Only a very few experiments ever work out—the majority are dismal failures. Once you understand this basic truth, there are essentially two ways to play the market. One approach is to buy new issues, that is newly listed shares with promotable stories, and hope for the best. It's a bit like playing darts blindfolded. The other strategy, and the more reliable one in the long run, is to short stocks that have already had a good run, knowing that the vast majority of them, with Newtonian inevitability, will eventually come down again. That's why I was so sure I couldn't lose." He shook his head ruefully. "Little did I know."

He paused and sipped his tea, his hand steadier now. "I'd decided to concentrate on companies in Charles Murray's stable. They'd generally done well in a poor market, owing in large part to Murray's abilities as a promoter, but based on my technical indicators I'd identified four stocks that I felt were due for significant pullbacks. Also, there'd been rumors on the street about him retiring, which had put additional pressure on the market. Anyway, I loaded up on the short side, but things very soon began to go wrong. One of his companies got some interesting drill results in Mexico last year. It was just my bloody luck. The rest of his stocks were swept along on the rising tide of euphoria.

"The thing is—and this is the strange part—they just kept going up for no obvious reason. I suspected that something had to be happening behind the scenes, but for the life of me I couldn't get to the bottom of it. I was getting calls from my broker twice a day to either put up more money or cover my positions and take the losses, neither of which I could afford to do. Eventually, I mortgaged my house and put everything I had into the market, still convinced that I'd be proven right in the end." He looked at Powell with an odd expression. "And I suppose I was, in a way."

Fear and greed, greed and fear. "Why did you come to Kinlochy?" Powell asked.

Sanders shrugged. "I had to know the truth. If there was something big in the works, I'd have no choice but to bail out and cut my losses. If, on the other hand, Murray's stocks were simply being driven by the usual promotional frenzy, I could afford to wait for the bubble to burst. So a couple of months ago I quit my job and began to work out a plan of action."

"That was a bit drastic, wasn't it, considering your financial position?"

"Look, I know what you're thinking. The fact is I had nothing more to lose. If I got wiped out, a regular salary would benefit only my ex-wife. Even if I got lucky and didn't lose my shirt, I wanted nothing more to do with the market. Either way, I intended to travel and freelance."

"Go on."

"As soon as I arrived in Kinlochy, I set myself up at the guesthouse and began to nose around. My intention was to spend a few days getting the lay of the land and then try to get an interview with Murray. I'd met him a few times in Vancouver, so I figured there was a good chance he'd agree to see me. When I saw Oliver Pickens in the pub I became more convinced than ever that something was up. You already know the rest."

"So you never did find out?"

Sanders shook his head.

"I suppose it's academic now. You got what you wanted, after all."

Sanders stared at Powell with an expression of disbelief. "Do I look happy?"

"Have you traded any shares since Murray's death?"

"What? No, of course not—I mean I've had other things on my mind. Call my broker if you don't believe me."

"I'll do that." Powell got abruptly to his feet. "We'll be in touch."

Barrett shook his head stubbornly. "You know it's not enough. There's not a shred of evidence that Sanders even talked to Murray, let alone killed him. Look, I'm not saying he couldn't have done it—I'm simply saying we don't have a case."

He glared at Powell with Cyclopsian intensity, his blind eye seemingly fixed on a point somewhere above and behind Powell's right shoulder. Powell resisted the temptation to look around.

"In fact, he's nowhere near the top of my list," Barrett continued.

Powell flushed. "Just for once, get to the bloody point and tell me what you really think."

Barrett exploded, "You want to know what I think? I think it's time we got on with the fucking job." He stormed out of the room.

Powell sat motionless while the minutes slowly passed. At one point he became dimly aware that PC Shand was asking if there was anything he needed. Finally, he was alone. He had felt like this before; times when he could barely bring himself to get out of bed and face what his life had become. Burnout is commonplace these days, nothing at all to worry about. Take these, a bit of rest, a change of scene, and you'll soon be right as rain. Strange simile, that. He swore violently to himself.

Dragging his mind kicking and screaming back to the task at hand, he knew now what had been bothering him—staring him in the face all along. He couldn't even begin to understand, but the unrelenting certainty of it crushed down on him. There was one more thing he had to do, still a faint hope, perhaps. He willed himself to move. He knew if he didn't, he'd be finished.

CHAPTER 17

Pinky Warburton was sitting alone in the lounge bar of the Salar Lodge sipping a sherry when Powell walked in and sat down.

"You know, Erskine, I'm going to miss this place."

"I know what you mean."

There was something in Powell's voice.

"Well, cheer up, you'll be back again next year."

"I don't know. A lot has happened."

"Nonsense. People will soon forget about Charles Murray. Things will be back to normal in no time at all. You'll see."

"What about you?"

"Oh, I'm a pretty resilient sort of chap. I'll get over it. Although I must admit I'll sleep better when the villain is brought to justice. By the way, any progress on that front?"

"Progress? I suppose you could say that."

Warburton smiled. "Is it classified information, old boy?"

"I stopped in at Grant's Tackle Shop on my way over

here. To pick up a pair of trout rods for Peter and David. Fishing is a good outlet for teenage boys, don't you think?"

"Never did us any harm."

"I'd decided on a pair of those custom rods that old Peter Grant builds," Powell continued in a monotone voice, "but I couldn't find any in the racks. There were plenty of Hardys, Bruce and Walkers, and even a few unmarked models, but none of Peter Grant's that I could see. When I inquired, the shop assistant informed me that Grant never signs his rods. The only identifying marks are the initials *P.G.* stamped on the reel seat."

There was a lengthy silence.

"I could have sworn," Warburton said eventually, "the poacher's rod—I was certain it was signed *Peter Grant* in India ink, just above the grip. Perhaps the trauma of recent events has impaired my memory." He shivered convincingly.

Powell stared at him, expressionless. "There never was a rod, was there, Pinky?"

"What the devil do you mean?"

"You made the whole thing up. The rod, the so-called attack, everything."

Warburton drew himself up indignantly. "If this is your idea of a joke, Erskine, I must say that it's in extremely poor taste."

"The joke's on me, I'd say."

"Are you seriously suggesting that I tried to drown myself as a lark?"

"No, not as a lark. To eliminate any possibility of suspicion coming your way. I think you simply misjudged the risk, as I did myself when I attempted to reenact the event. In any case, your performance was most convincing. You certainly had me fooled. Although I wasn't in the best position to be entirely objective."

Warburton shook his head in disbelief. "Erskine, we've known each other for nearly thirty years. Do you realize what you're saying? I can't possibly see how my not remembering what can only be characterized as a trivial detail has led you to make these extraordinary and hurtful allegations."

Powell spoke abstractedly, as if thinking aloud. "Right from the start it didn't make any sense. Why would anybody attempt to commit a murder over a fishing rod? The implied connection with Murray's death served only to cloud the waters. I can see now that was the whole point. To lay a false scent. Ironically, it was another fishing rod that finally put me on to it."

"I must say, Erskine," Warburton said irritably, "these cryptic allusions of yours elude me. Would you mind terribly getting to the point?"

"It's been staring me in the face all along, but I couldn't, or wouldn't, see it. Why would you, after bringing in this rod as you claim, wade out to a dangerous perch on a slippery rock to examine it? You could have done it safely on the bank where you'd just laid down your own rod."

Warburton sighed. "I was hoping it wouldn't come to this," he said. "But you know as well as I do that the evidence against me is circumstantial. None of it would stand up in court. And before you judge me, you should consider the real villain in this piece. Charles Murray was a scoundrel of the highest order. He richly deserved everything he got. Do you realize how many lives he ruined?" He searched Powell's face for a glimmer of understanding. "I'll tell you everything. Just promise me you'll keep an open mind."

"You know I can't promise you anything."

"Then I'll have to take my chances." He hesitated for a moment and then seemed to make up his mind. "You've heard about the Warburton troubles. I've never told you or anyone else how my father lost the family fortune, or what was left of it. I suppose I find it too embarrassing to talk about, although, God knows, I think about it constantly. Several years ago, Father was introduced to Charles Murray at his club by a mutual acquaintance. Murray was in London promoting his latest mining venture. It must have been quite a sales pitch." He laughed bitterly. "The old man fell for it, hook, line, and sinker. A private placement to the tune of a half million pounds. Predictably, the pot at the end of the rainbow never materialized and Father's so-called investment ended up as so much worthless paper. You know the rest."

"That was a long time ago, Pinky."

"The bastard ruined my life and I never forgave him for it. I swore I'd get even. I've been planning it for years, as a matter of fact." He leaned forward, visibly animated now. "One day I was checking the estate listings on the office computer when I noticed that Castle Glyn was up for sale. I was aware that Murray had purchased the place last year and I saw my chance. Almost without effort the outline of a plan began to take shape in my mind. I remembered that you came up here each spring and I reckoned that an invitation to join you for a spot of salmon fishing would provide me with the perfect cover. After all, who would suspect an old mate of yours of anything untoward?"

"You took advantage," Powell said quietly.

"I know it sounds a bit mercenary, old chap, but I'm sure you can appreciate that I needed to keep my eye on the ball. Now where was I? Oh, yes. After you'd done your bit, I rang Murray up and told him that I had a prospective client but wished to view the property myself first. We agreed to meet on Monday, the day before I was scheduled to arrive at the Salar Lodge." Warburton leaned back and smiled. "It went more smoothly than I could have imagined, although there were moments, I can tell you. If I'd known you were going to arrive a day early—well, I don't know what I'd have done. But it's all water under the bridge, in a manner of speaking." He eyed Powell shrewdly. "I could use another sherry. How about you?"

"I think not."

Warburton shrugged. "You may be surprised to hear this, Erskine, but I didn't really have a game plan. I intended to play it more or less by ear. Originally I thought I'd have to invent some pretext or other to lure Murray away from Castle Glyn. That wasn't necessary, as it turned out. He was most cooperative, I'll give him that."

Although there was no outward sign of it, Powell was engaged in a fierce inner struggle to stem the flood of emotions that threatened to overwhelm him. *I mustn't lose control, not now,* he thought. He spoke slowly, as if in a trance, "I must caution you, Pinky—"

"Now, Erskine, we needn't bother with the formalities," Warburton interjected smoothly. He seemed almost eager to continue. "I called Murray as soon as I arrived in Kinlochy. He suggested that I drive out to Castle Glyn that afternoon. He quite conveniently mentioned that he was alone, so I would be free to have a good look around. When I arrived, it was all hail fellow, well met." Warburton's expression suddenly darkened. "Little did he know." He drained his glass with a convulsive gulp. "He gave me the grand tour and all I could think about was the injustice of it all—Warburton money had helped pay for that pile. Then he suggested we nip down to the Old Bridge for a spot of fishing before dark. As I'm sure you can imagine, sport was the last thing on my mind, but he'd obviously had a few drinks by then and wouldn't take no for an answer."

"So it was you," Powell said numbly, "fishing above the Old Bridge with the single-handed rod."

Warburton nodded. "He lent it to me. He didn't even have a proper salmon rod."

Powell swore violently, causing Warburton to start. "What a bloody fool I've been!"

"How do you think *I* felt?" Warburton said indignantly. "Spotting you up on the bridge like that and praying that you wouldn't recognize me?"

Warburton's words echoed strangely in Powell's head, as if they were being shouted from a great distance. He couldn't sort out whether he was more angry at Pinky for so callously betraying him, or at himself for refusing to acknowledge the truth for so long. Barrett knew. He was certain of that now.

"It was a bit tense, I can tell you," Warburton was saying. "But when you turned away I knew that I was going to pull it off." He removed a silk handkerchief from the breast pocket of his jacket and dabbed daintily at his brow. "When we got back to the house," he continued, "it was getting late. Murray insisted on fixing supper and

I had no choice but to humor him. Frankfurters and crisps with cold beer," he added parenthetically, pulling a face. "Time was running out and I was madly trying to formulate some sort of plan of attack when, out of the blue, he suggested that we drive into Kinlochy for a drink. I leapt at the chance and offered to take my Land Rover. It was a way to get him away from Castle Glyn. I just had to make certain that I wasn't seen with him."

"What time did you leave Castle Glyn?" Powell heard himself ask.

"Going on ten, give or take a few minutes."

Powell's attention wandered to the large stone fireplace that took up most of the wall behind Warburton. Something Pinky had said had triggered an association. On the mantelshelf was a bronze casting of a leaping salmon, frozen in space and time by the sculptor and freed for eternity from its watery prison. *Salar,* the leaper.

"As we drove," Warburton was saying, "Murray's behavior changed. Previously his manner could be described as one of boisterous good humor, enhanced no doubt by his state of inebriation, but as we neared our destination he became sullen. He wasn't entirely coherent, but he did say something about settling scores with that son of a bitch at the Salar Lodge. My original intention had been to stop at some conveniently secluded location along the way and, well, do what needed to be done. But as Murray railed against Bob, an alternate course of action began to take shape in the old think box. Let him be seen raving drunkenly in public—with yours truly remaining discreetly in the background, of course—before falling victim to some unfortunate mishap. So I was more than willing to oblige when he insisted that I take him to the Salar Lodge."

Powell had to suppress a grudging admiration for the sheer audacity of Pinky's plan. "Didn't it occur to you that you might just bump into me at the hotel?"

Warburton looked sadly at Powell, as if profoundly disappointed. "Erskine, really! I considered that possibility, of course. I would simply have had to abort the mission and fabricate some logical explanation for being there. However, I did take precautions. You may recall that it was a filthy night and the streets were more or less deserted. When we got to the Salar Lodge I dropped Murray off and then parked at the rear of the car park. When he emerged from the hotel about ten minutes later, I waited to make sure that he was alone before driving over to pick him up, stopping short so I couldn't be seen from the front entrance. He was rather annoyed at having to walk over to the car in the rain."

"I can see you had it all worked out."

"The rest was easy. As we drove toward town along the stretch of road beside the river, I had a flash of inspiration. After checking to make sure there was no traffic, I pulled off to the side. I told him that I needed to relieve myself. He muttered something about needing a piss, too. There was a short path through the trees to the river. I let him go first. As he was undoing his fly I picked up a rock and let him have it from behind, then I rolled him over the bank into the water. It would look like a tragic accident. I then drove to Grantown and took a hotel room for the night. The next day I appeared on schedule at the Salar Lodge." As if finally unburdened, he heaved a huge sigh and sat placidly in silence.

Powell could think of nothing to say, only of what he had to do. Eventually he spoke, as if to distract himself, "And the rod?"

Warburton smiled. "As you guessed, a ruse to direct any possible suspicion in the direction of Arthur's poacher and away from yours truly. I knew that you didn't believe Murray's death had been an accident. But I can see now that my little diversionary tactic was a mistake. 'Oh what tangled webs we weave' and whatnot."

"Bob Whitely's van was seen parked at the Old Bridge shortly before your little accident on Wednesday. Did you see him?"

"He stopped by to see me. He wanted my opinion on the market value of the Salar Lodge, that's all."

Powell barely held his temper. "Did you at any time consider the possibility that you might be implicating an innocent person?"

"Actually, the thought never occurred to me," Warburton replied blandly.

So it has come to this, Powell thought. He felt empty, drained of any capacity for action. "Why, Pinky? Why did you do it?"

"I've told you why."

"But cold-blooded murder?"

"I prefer to think of it as the extermination of a particularly odious variety of parasite."

"But how does it change things? You've been managing all right."

"That's easy for you to say," Warburton snapped, his face turning a bright pink. "I'm sorry, Erskine," he added quickly. "That was unfair; you've been most understanding. But you have no idea what it's like selling shirts to tourists in Jermyn Street. You of all people should know that I wasn't cut out to be a boxwallah. To answer your question—no, it doesn't entirely make up for what I've been through. But it bloody well helps."

"The point is you got caught."

"I guess I did at that, that is if you feel compelled to do your duty." He hesitated. "But of course you do. Mind you, I could deny that this conversation ever took place."

"Yes, I suppose you could."

Warburton smiled wearily. "Don't worry, old chap, I'll go quietly." He stood up. "I'll just collect my things."

Powell nodded. He sat immobilized. The minutes stretched out slowly. His consciousness was focused on the bronze salmon above the fireplace. *Salar,* the leaper. He blinked slowly. The figure seemed to shift and change like a hallucinogenic mandala. Suddenly he leapt to his feet. "Christ Almighty!"

Powell drove like a man possessed. When he arrived at the Old Bridge he found Warburton leaning over the parapet, gazing intently at the river below. The water had dropped considerably over the past week and numerous boulders were now exposed, breaking the current into a swirling pattern of complex vortices. The sky was a dull gunmetal gray and there wasn't a breath of air. Somewhere nearby, a raven croaked harshly.

Powell called out. Warburton turned and raised his arm. Powell approached with careful, deliberate steps. He stopped about ten paces away.

"Come with me, Pinky, and I'll do what I can."

Warburton began to move slowly toward him. He

shook his head. "It's no good, Erskine. Prison food wouldn't agree with me."

Instinctively, Powell braced himself. Warburton turned, took several quick steps, and then, before Powell could react, he vaulted with surprising agility over the parapet, landing, after what seemed like an interminable interval, with a sickening thud on the rocks below. Powell rushed to the low stone wall. He watched as Warburton's body drifted downstream with the current, deflecting crazily off one boulder and then another, as if in play in some ghastly pinball game.

EPILOGUE

The events of the past few days were little more than a jumbled blur in Powell's mind. There had been statements to be given and arrangements to be made, the calls to Marion, and the inevitable bouts of commiseration with Barrett in the lounge bar of the Salar Lodge. But he ruthlessly suppressed any more distinct impressions. There would be time enough for postmortems later. Having only a few remaining hours in Kinlochy, he'd managed to slip away and wander down to the river, rod in hand, with no particular intention other than to get away by himself. Away from the well meaning but oppressive ministrations of Nigel and Ruby and even Alex, who had been exhibiting disturbing tendencies of a mother hen of late.

The morning was bright and transparent and hinted of summer. He stopped at a likely looking pool and put up his rod. Wading in at the head, he began to switch out line, savoring the sensuous bend and spring of the old cane rod. Heaving as hard as he dared, he cast a full thirty yards of line down and across the pool. After the current

227

had pulled the line around to a point directly below him, he took a step downstream, lifted his fly to the surface with the long rod, swept the line upstream and then out over the river again in a graceful rolling movement. In this manner he slowly worked his way downstream to the bottom end of the pool where the river narrowed and drew into the broken reach below. He let his fly hang motionless in the rough water for a few minutes, surmising that on such a warm, sunny morning a fish would feel more secure in the tumble of the riffle than in the breathless transparency of the pool. He began to reel in his line. So much for that little theory.

Then, without warning, his rod bowed sharply and a twisting slab of silver erupted from the water, scattering spray like a shower of molten diamonds. His reel screamed as the fish ran downstream, aided by the pull of the current. He scrambled ashore and began to play the fish, giving it line when it wanted to run and applying pressure when it tried to rest. Although there were some anxious moments, for one of the few times in his life he never once doubted the outcome. He maneuvered the salmon into a position opposite him and slightly upstream, so that the fish was forced to work against both the current and the pull of the line. It quickly tired and Powell was able to draw it into shallow water over a shingled bar.

It was a lovely creature, weighing perhaps fifteen pounds, silver bright and throbbing with the urgency of life, aware at some primal level that its predestined journey home from the Greenland seas to the spawning bed of its birth had been cruelly interrupted. It was the largest salmon he had ever caught and, as he bent down to dispatch it, he couldn't help wondering what Barrett would say. He lifted the staghorn priest above his head, hesitated, then lowered his hand.

The fish lay quietly on its side, its gill covers barely moving. Using a pair of pliers, Powell removed the tiny double hook from the fish's jaw and then, cradling its body in one arm while gripping the narrow wrist of the fish's tail tightly with the other hand, waded into the river. When he was knee-deep, he carefully lowered the salmon into the water with its head facing into the current. He worked the fish back and forth with a gentle, rocking motion, causing water to flow over its gills. After a few moments he felt the first faint stirring, as if the great fish were awakening from a dream and then, with a powerful thrust of its tail, it was free.

Powell watched, his mind empty, as the salmon, reflecting sunlight like a mirror, turned away with the current and slowly disappeared into the river's blue embrace.

Don't miss the next Erskine Powell mystery:

MALICE IN CORNWALL
by Graham Thomas

Coming this summer from Ivy Books.

For a sneak preview, read on . . .

The moon was large that night and so was she. She had left her friends in the pub and set out alone along the beach humming the latest Beatles tune to herself. The lights of the pub and the din of revelry—snatches of laughter, the faint tintinnabulation of clinking glasses on the patio, and the beat of the music—dwindled in the distance. She thought about her boyfriend back there drinking himself into a stupor. Their romantic week-end at the seaside hadn't exactly turned out that way; he'd be no good at all to her later, but then he wasn't much good at the best of times, and she wasn't into alcohol. Screw *him*, she was having a gas!

She kicked off her shoes and ran along the beach, heart pounding at the rush of air into her open mouth, her long hair flying like a white mare's tail in the moonlight. She experienced the sharp texture of sand beneath her feet, the cooling breeze against her skin, the iodine smell of the sea. She spread her arms wide, shafts of golden light emanating from her fingertips, encircling the moon with a writhing aurora. "God, I'm stoned!" she shouted to anyone who cared to listen.

The sea whispered to her, drawing her closer to the water's edge. The sand had given way to shingle, so she slowed, prancing gingerly amongst the stones; patches of slimy sea wrack squished between her toes and she wished that she had kept her shoes. Her eyes widened. The beach was moving as if a million chitinous creatures were swarming over it and there was an acrid smell in the air. I mustn't freak, she told herself.

She stared in wonder at her body; it was bathed in a suffusive light that seemed to originate beneath her skin, perhaps from the intricate pattern of blue-wire veins she could trace with her finger. The light expanded around her and she was no longer sure what was inside or outside, or whether the distinction even had any meaning.

The waves hissed and clawed at the rocks with white-foam fingers. She could sense the rise and fall of luminous seaweed in the bay and myriad cold eyes searching the deeps. She knew somehow that she was not alone.

She couldn't understand why she hadn't noticed it before. Shimmering in the moonlight like a wondrous mirror, a large pool filled by the rising tide was now isolated by a circle of rocks jutting up like broken black teeth. She felt as if she were floating above its quicksilver surface. She tried to focus at a point beyond her reflection to see what lay at the heart of it. There was something there, just beyond the limits of her perception, something elusive, insubstantial, yet deeply meaningful and transcendent.

After what seemed like hours, an image slowly began to resolve itself beneath the surface of the water. A young girl perhaps sixteen or seventeen stared back at her with incredulous eyes, pupils dilated like her own, skin like alabaster and a cloud of dark hair drifting around her face as if softly stirred by her breath. Except how could she be breathing?

I'm really tripping now, she thought wonderingly. She moved closer. The girl in the pool was naked like some lovely mermaid, wearing only a choker, a black satin ribbon encircling her slender neck with an ivory cameo in the center.

She stared at this simple if incongruous adornment, fascinated. The choker was oddly frayed at the edges, and it occurred to her that something was not quite right. She was coming down fast.

She suddenly realized that it wasn't a choker at all, but rather a deep dark gash, the severed trachea exposed like some obscene white hosepipe. The throat had been neatly cut.

They could hear her screaming all the way back at the pub.

MALICE IN CORNWALL
by Graham Thomas

Coming this summer from Ivy Books.